Bend it like Baxter

by

Jim Orr

Jim Orr
Copyright c 2017
All Rights Reserved

Act 1

Scene 1   Horseshoe Bar, Glasgow (October 2017)
Scene 2   Horseshoe Bar, Glasgow (13 April 1967)
Scene 3   Train, Glasgow to London Sleeper
Scene 4   Café, London (14 April 1967)
Scene 5   Photo Studio, London

Act 2

Scene 1   Nightclub, London
Scene 2   Bed and Breakfast, London (15 April 1967)
Scene 3   Wembley, London
Scene 4   Wembley, London (post-match)
Scene 5   Horseshoe Bar, Glasgow (October 2017)

ACT 1, SCENE 1 - HORSESHOE BAR, GLASGOW (OCTOBER 2017)

LX:	Stage left

Jimmy (82) has just returned from the funeral of his best mate (Jack). He is wearing a black suit, he takes off his tie and sits at the bar.

BARMAID
Alright Jimmy, how did the funeral go?

OLD JIMMY
Not much of a turn out hen, then again at our age, not many of us left. Jack didn't have any family. What a bloody week eh, first that shambles in Slovenia, now this.

BARMAID
You must be really upset. Here, whisky, on the house.

OLD JIMMY
Aye hen, devastated, close to tears. I mean we were one up at half time. Forty five minutes from a play off.

BARMAID
What?

OLD JIMMY
Slovenia, were you not listening?

BARMAID
What are you on about?

OLD JIMMY
Only forty five minutes from a play off. Christ, I spend longer than that these days trying to have a pee.

BARMAID
Your best pal has just died and you're prattling on about the daft football.

OLD JIMMY
That's twenty years since we qualified, twenty years. I was 62 then, in my prime with a fully functioning bladder. Twenty years. Look at me now, a doddery old man.

BARMAID
Doddery, old, you, no! What did he die of?

OLD JIMMY

Hope.

BARMAID

Hope?

OLD JIMMY

Watching Scotland, it's the hope that kills you, that's what happened. I mean we knew straight away, start of the second half, weren't at the races. Then bang, bang, 2-1 down and you just knew, that was it. Then Snodgrass scores in the last minute and Jack starts shouting and bawling.

BARMAID

Shouting and bawling?

OLD JIMMY

Aye, well I thought he was just excited at the goal, turned out he was having a heart attack.

BARMAID

So, what did you do?

OLD JIMMY

Nothing, I was too wrapped up in the game. Turned round after the final whistle and he was slumped in the chair, dead.

BARMAID

For Christ's sake.

OLD JIMMY

One goal, that's all we needed. Aye, it's the hope that kills you right enough! How did it come to this?

BARMAID

Come to what?

OLD JIMMY

We keep getting our arses, well and truly felt by these wee countries. Are you not listening? I mean, I don't even know where Slovenia is.

BARMAID

East.

OLD JIMMY

Past Edinburgh?

BARMAID

Aye, turn left past Edinburgh, that's you, Slovenia.

OLD JIMMY
Wouldn't have happened back in the day hen. Not that they existed back in the day.

BARMAID
Who's that then?

OLD JIMMY
Slovenia! We had that Communist bloc back then, the good old days. Then all these new countries spring up from nowhere whose sole purpose seems to be mucking up our chances of qualifying for major tournaments.

BARMAID
Major tournaments, aye.

OLD JIMMY
If it's not the Slovenia, it's the Ukraine or it's the Slovakia or it's the Lithuania and don't get me started on that Georgia.

BARMAID
Georgia, aye what she like?

OLD JIMMY
Nothing they like better than putting us out on our arses every chance they get. The tournaments we'd have qualified for if they clowns had left that Berlin Wall alone! No, they had to knock it down and bam, twenty years.

BARMAID
The wall, aye.

OLD JIMMY
Know what you're thinking hen, daft old bugger pining for the good old days that didn't actually exist. Back in the day, back in the day hen, well, football was football, the beautiful game. Not like nowadays. Where are your players, I mean proper players?

BARMAID
Is that wee Messi not meant to be the best player ever?

OLD JIMMY
Messi! Messi! Christ, he's only got one foot. In my day, if I was up against Messi, I'd jockey him, push him onto his right, he doesn't have a right foot.

BARMAID
Who did you play for?

OLD JIMMY
Played a bit of amateur back in the day hen, good level mind. Couple of our lads had trials with Stenhousemuir, that's how good we were. Although they didn't get signed!

BARMAID
You'd have taken care of Messi?

OLD JIMMY
'Though shalt not pass', my motto, so if your Messi tried to pass me, bam, down the wee bugger would go. Wouldn't have lasted two minutes in the Glasgow Corporation Amateur League (pauses) Third Division. I'd have crippled him.

BARMAID
Aye, beautiful game right enough, back in the day!

OLD JIMMY
Back in the day an ordinary working man could afford to go the football. That England match a few months ago, £50 a ticket! Not on my pension. But back in the day, never missed an England match at Hampden and Wembley. Aye Wembley, me and Jack, God rest him, every second year, the Wembley week-end, biggest match in the world in they days. Saved for two years then 30, 40, 50 thousand of the troops would head down to the Big Smoke. Was like the Fair Fortnight, Christmas and Hogmanay rolled into one.

BARMAID
The fair what?

OLD JIMMY
Wait to I show you this.

| VFX: | **Jim Baxter with the two fans** |

OLD JIMMY
There you go, man in the middle, know who that is?

BARMAID
Him getting strangled, haven't a Scooby?

OLD JIMMY
Needs no introduction, I'll introduce him anyway (slowly) James Curran Baxter.

BARMAID

Never heard of him.

OLD JIMMY

Slim Jim Baxter, one of the greatest Scottish players of all time, if not <u>the</u> greatest player. Stanley, they called him, after the comedian Stanley Baxter.

BARMAID

Comedian, was he?

OLD JIMMY

I'll 'comedian' you. Wand for a left foot, put a ball on a sixpence. Never used his right foot, left was that good.

BARMAID

Just like Messi?

OLD JIMMY

Aye well you might think I'm being a bit hypocritical when I had a go at your wee Messi for being one footed but I have a good excuse...I'm old! When you get to my age you can spout any old pish and get away with it, one of the few advantages of getting old!

BARMAID

(sarcastically) You, old, no!

OLD JIMMY

Anyway, clock the two either side of Slim Jim, handsome fellas in their best suits. Any idea who they are?

BARMAID

You and your pal?

OLD JIMMY

No, haven't a bloody clue, always wanted to find out, thought you might know them!

BARMAID

Aye, they're in here all the time they two!

OLD JIMMY

That match, 50 years ago, Christ seems like yesterday. What a weekend that was, Wembley '67, the greatest Scotland match of all time. You see Jack and I <u>were</u> at that match. We <u>were</u> on that pitch at the end of the match. That should have been us in that photo, could have been us but (pauses) draw up a pew.

| LX: | Lights down |

| VFX: | The Happening by The Supremes |

ACT 1 SCENE 2 - HORSESHOE BAR, GLASGOW (13 APRIL 1967, 21:30)

LX:	Centre stage

We are transported back to April 1967. Old Jimmy (wearing a cardigan) will occasionally comment on proceedings as he observes his younger self and Jack on their Wembley trip.

Jimmy (32) is sitting at a table and is wearing a smart suit, shirt and tie plus tartan scarf and tammy His best mate Jack (also 32), wearing a crumpled suit, shirt tail hanging out and loose tie plus tartan scarf and tammy, has just returned from the bar with a full tray of beers.

OLD JIMMY (NARRATING)
The match, as usual, was on the Saturday, we'd normally travel down by train the day before but I was sick, fed up with the crowds. Could never get a seat, all crushed and nutters pishing in your pockets, no, really, clatty bastards! Trains with toilets was a luxury back then! So, I thought, last train on the Thursday night, a kip on the train and a wee wander around the football grounds in London on the Friday before heading to the usual haunts at night.

We were in the Horseshoe, quarter to ten, 'last orders gentlemen please' shouted the barmaid. Pubs shut at 10:00 in they days, Christ, the young ones are just going out then!

Was just hoping my bladder would survive another Wembley week-end!

BARMAID
Last orders gentlemen please.

JIMMY
Took you?

OLD JIMMY (NARRATING)
(pointing to his younger self) Scrubbed up well back in the day, eh?

JACK
There you go Jimbo, triple round, going to be a long night.

JIMMY
You need to cut down on the bevvy.

JACK

Helps me relax.

JIMMY

You don't work, live with your old dear and spend all your time at the bookies or in the pub or chasing women.

JACK

And that's not stressful? Alright for you, engaged, fancy new house, inside toilet and a good job with prospects, you've nothing to worry about. Do you know how stressful the 'women chasing' is these days? Not like it used to be, a couple of dances and next thing you're on for your Nat King. Last time I tried to pick up a bird she asked me what star sign I was to check if we were compatible, whatever that means. Whole different ball game these days, the 'women chasing'. I'm a Pisces by the way.

JIMMY

When was the last time you worked?

JACK

Not many jobs for the likes of me.

JIMMY

What, lazy bastards?

JACK

Just waiting for the right opportunity.

JIMMY

Heard the labour exchange invited you to their last Christmas party you've been signing on that long!

JACK

It's because I'm a Pisces, hold on, (takes a piece of paper out of his pocket) deep thinkers, weigh up all the options before they act, not to be rushed.

JIMMY

So, all Pisces are lazy bastards?

JACK

It's all in the stars.

JIMMY

Listen to 'Harry the Hippy', you'll be turning vegetarian next.

JACK

What's one of them when it's at home?

JIMMY
They don't eat anything that's been killed.

JACK
Cannibals?

JIMMY
They're the opposite of the vegetarians. I was reading that sausages are made from pig's testicles.

JACK
Bollocks!

JIMMY
Exactly.

JACK
(thinks) How come you get flat sausages, if they were made from pig's balls there would be wee bits sticking out, eh, smart arse?

JIMMY
It's all processed.

JACK
Wouldn't get many sausages from pig's balls, well unless they were big pigs (holds out his hands). Then again you might get a big pig with wee balls or a wee pig with big balls!

OLD JIMMY (NARRATING)
As I struggled to answer that profound question this big bloke in a sheepskin coat appeared and lifted Jack's feet off the table.

TAM
Sunshine, if you don't want my size 14s splitting your jacksie in half, I would suggest you move your filthy feet.

JACK
Sorry mate, didn't realise this was your pub!

TAM
I'm not your mate.

JACK
Who pissed on your chips (pauses) mate?

JIMMY

Jack, leave it!

TAM
(to Jack) Look sunshine, never trouble trouble until trouble troubles you, got it? Now let's see if we can behave in a more civilised manner. You wouldn't want to have an unfortunate accident and miss the match, would you?

JIMMY
No, no we wouldn't.

TAM
Personally, I think we'll get horsed but it's good for business. Thousands of mug punters, pished out their skulls with two year's dosh burning a hole in their skyrockets.

JIMMY
What business are you in Mr, eh...?

TAM
Tunnock, Tam Tunnock.

JACK
'The Tea-cake'!

TAM
<u>Mister</u> Tunnock sunshine. Your mother not teach you manners?

JACK
Sorry, <u>Mister</u> Tunnock, thought I recognised you from the papers, you got off with that murder at the High Court yesterday.

TAM
'Not proven' are the words your limited vocabulary is searching for.

JACK
But you stabbed a bloke to death.

TAM
Fell on my knife.

JACK
20 times?

TAM
These things happen, look, I'm a respectable businessman, my card. (gives card to Jimmy)

JIMMY
Gentlemen's clubs. (gives card to Jack)

JACK
Is that strip clubs, nudey women?

TAM
The London, you're in for a bit of shock boys, changed quite a bit since the last Wembley. Then it was all dancing chimneysweeps and feed the birds tuppence a bag, now it it's all love, peace, drugs and see through knickers.

JACK
Ya dancer!

TAM
All good for business.

Tam goes into his briefcase and passes a magazine to Jack.

TAM
For my special clientele.

JACK
What?

TAM
£1.

JACK
For a scuddy mag?

TAM
Well it's not the People's Friend! Straight from Copenhagen, our Scandinavian cousins are a bit more, how can I put it, experimental!

JACK
(to Jimmy) Give him £1.

JIMMY
What!

JACK
You'll get it back. When do I not pay you back?

JIMMY
You never pay me back.

OLD JIMMY (NARRATING)

I give the big man £1, Jack opens the magazine and spits his beer all over me.

JIMMY
What the f'!

JACK
Look at this cow!

JIMMY
Not your type?

JACK
No, this nutter is doing it with a cow (to Tam) Copenhagen, what they just jump into the fields and do it with cows?

TAM
No, they wine and dine them first, what do you think sunshine?

JACK
I'm definitely becoming a vegetarian! (showing Jimmy the picture) Look at that.

OLD JIMMY (NARRATING)
After seeing that image, this vegetarian stuff started to make a lot of sense. Never mind don't eat anything that's been killed, don't eat anything that might have been shagged by some nutter in Copenhagen before it's been killed! Never touched Danish bacon again!

JACK
(handing the magazine to Jimmy) Here.

JIMMY
You're alright, I'll wait for the film.

TAM
Well if that's what floats your boat. (goes into briefcase) There you go boys, (holds up a rectangular box) film cassettes.

JACK
What?

TAM
Cinema of the future. Adult films for the connoisseur. This one is called, eh, (checks the label) 'The Real Snow White'.

                         JACK
What!

                         TAM
One woman living with seven men, join the dots sunshine.

                         JIMMY
Snow White and the dwarves were...

                    OLD JIMMY (NARRATING)
Disney make sense, boom, boom!

                         JACK
They're dwarves?

                         TAM
Still men, men with manly urges, working men, hi ho, hi ho, it's off to work they go.

                         JIMMY
He's not familiar with that song!

                         JACK
Christ, what's next, The *Real* Broons, The *Real* Oor Wullie?

                         JIMMY
Oor Wullie, your Wullie, a'body's Wullie!

                         JACK
Jings, crivvens, help ma boaby!

Jack turns the pages while moving the magazine horizontally and vertically.

                         JACK
So, what goes on in these strip clubs?

                         TAM
Gentlemen's clubs.

Tam whispers in Jack's ear and he spits out his drink over Jimmy.

                         JACK
Never!

                         TAM
That's just for starters.

Tam whispers in Jack's ear and he spits out his drink over Jimmy again.

JACK
Ping pong balls! Christ! I'll never be able to play table tennis again. Your Annie would be the talk of the Steamie if she got up to some of this stuff.

JIMMY
She doesn't go to the Steamie.

JACK
Talk of the laundrette then! The London, can't wait. (rubs hands) Permissive society, hot pants, top-less waitresses.

TAM
Don't forget 'The Pill' son, wonder of modern science.

JACK
(rubs hands again) Aye, no more jonneeeees!

TAM
Stops the ball getting in the net if you know what I mean! (puts both hands up to indicate 'stop')

JIMMY
Like a goalie?

TAM
Exactly sunshine.

JIMMY
Like Ronnie Simpson?

TAM
Aye.

JACK
Or Frank Haffey?

TAM
Aye, (thinks) no, no bloody Frank Haffey, after letting in they nine goals, Christ, if the 'Pill' was like Frank Haffey most women would be up the duff!

JIMMY
There was a programme on BBC2 the other night about the pill.

JACK

My old dear doesn't let me watch that channel, too much dirty stuff. When something a bit dodgy comes on she switches it off, blames the aerial! One night she threw a towel over my head, told me to dry my hair and it wasn't even wet!

OLD JIMMY (NARRATING)
Only three channels back then, some of the old programmes are still on, eh Doctor Who for one. Never understood him, can travel back in time, think of the good he could have done to change history for the better, too busy arseing about with Daleks and Cybermen! Could have killed Hitler before he came to power. Geoff Hurst as well

JACK
Let's give the football grounds a body serve, strip clubs, come on?

OLD JIMMY (NARRATING)
Had Friday all planned. A wee wander around the football grounds, Highbury, Stamford Bridge, White Hart Line, had the underground routes all worked out but with The Tea-cake mentioning nudey clubs, knew where 'head the baw' would want to go.

Always wanted to see White Hart Lane, had a soft spot for the Spurs. They were at home that Saturday, aye, Spurs playing at the same time as the England match, never happen nowadays.

JIMMY
Spurs are at home on Saturday, we might see Gilzean or Mackay training.

OLD JIMMY (NARRATING)
Shows you the players we had to pick from in they days, Dave Mackay, one of the greatest Scottish football players of all time, not picked for Wembley '67!

JACK
Why is Mackay not playing for us on Saturday?

TAM
(slowly) Dave Mackay, now he is one hard, hard bastard, met him a few times and do you know what?

JACK
What?

TAM

(slowly) He is one hard, hard bastard, takes no prisoners Mackay. He's not playing against that mob on Saturday! Stevie Wonder picking the team? Who's playing?

JACK
Well Gemmell, Greig, McKinnon...

TAM
Hard bastards.

JACK
McCreadie...

TAM
Bloody psycho McCreadie is, they English fannies will not be taking liberties with those boys. Is that the time? Need to love you and leave, duty calls.

Tam drinks up and leaves. Jack throws the magazine to Jimmy.

JACK
There you go.

JACK
That's what you'll be missing once you're married. Well known fact, once you're married, your sex life finished. You <u>really sure</u> you want to go through with <u>it</u>?

JIMMY
You're my best man, you're not meant to be throwing temptation in my face, get behind me Satan! Annie is my soul-mate. She's the one, the one I'm going to spend all my life with.

Jack thinks about this for a few seconds. Jimmy picks up the magazine and turns it horizontal and vertical.

JACK
What about Saturdays, the football?

JIMMY
(pauses) Of course, we'll still have Saturdays, the football.

JACK
Wednesdays, mid-week matches?

JIMMY
(pauses) Aye, of course mid-week matches, obviously.

JACK

Friday nights, the pub, boy's night out?

JIMMY

Eh aye, aye Fridays, can't miss boys night out.

JACK

Ok, if that's your decision, I'll respect it!

OLD JIMMY (NARRATING)

So that was me setting Jack straight, I felt better that he knew exactly where we stood!

JACK

Thought I had found my soul mate once, wasn't to be.

JIMMY

You, soul mate!

JACK

I was married.

JIMMY

Shite, we've known each other since we were kids. I think I'd know if you'd been married.

JACK

1955, end of my National Service, never spoken about it. Didn't last long.

JIMMY

How long?

JACK

A day (pauses) well half a day. 2 April 1955, London registry office. An English rose, Emily, my soul mate, or so I thought.

JIMMY

On you go.

JACK

After the reception, went to Wembley, England match, with her four brothers and her old man.

JIMMY

What happened?

JACK

Stanley f'n Matthews is what happened, ripped the bloody pish out of us.

JIMMY
7-2 game?

JACK
Aye, seven f'n two and her old man and brothers are giving me dogs abuse, jumping about like arseholes, Rule Britannia and all that shite so I thought, stuff that for a game of soldiers, I'm up the road.

OLD JIMMY (NARRATING)
Any man would do the same, mental cruelty they call that these days!

JACK
So, I know just how our Anglos will be feeling on Saturday.

JIMMY
Back page of the Citizen said Denis might be injured.

JACK
Christ that's all we need. Denis knows the score with that mob. Him, wee Billy, Slim Jim and the other Anglos, they'll have had to listen to all their shite since last summer. He'll make it, don't you worry.

JIMMY
Baxter! Think his best days are behind him.

OLD JIMMY (NARRATING)
Wasn't sure about Slim Jim after he broke his leg a couple of years earlier but Jack was still his number one fan.

JACK
He'll still do them, don't you worry.

JIMMY
This is a good England team.

JACK
No such thing as a good England team. A 'lucky' England team, a 'jammy so and so' team, a 'cheating bastards' team but no such thing as a good England team.

JIMMY
They've a few good players, the Charlton's?

JACK
Baldy Bain and his big, ugly sister!

JIMMY

Nobby Stiles?

JACK

Son of Frankenstein!

JIMMY

Alan Ball?

JACK

Jimmy Clitheroe? They're all shite, only beat us once in the last five years.

OLD JIMMY (NARRATING)

Then I made the mistake of mentioning the WC, no, not water closet, if only. The World Cup! Jack had been counting down the days to this Wembley since that fateful day the previous summer.

JIMMY

World cup winners!

JACK

My arse that mob won it. They stole it, they know they stole it and they know that we know they stole it. We'll put them in their place, no danger. And after the match it'll be "cheer up Alf Ramsay, oh what can it mean, to be a sad English bastard and a shite football team". (although not a football song at the time, Scotland fans sing this today to the tune of Daydream Believer, inserting the name of the current England manager).

OLD JIMMY (NARRATING)

Years ahead of his time that boy!

LX:	**Lights down**

VFX:	**Daydream Believer by The Monkees**

ACT 1 SCENE 3 – TRAIN, GLASGOW TO LONDON SLEEPER (22:30)

LX:	Centre stage

OLD JIMMY (NARRATING)
On the overnight Glasgow to London train, wandering down the corridor. We were happy, merry men just like Robin Hood's chinas. We'd had a few swallys, were having a sing song. (singing) 'We shall not, we shall not be moved, not by the Welsh, the Irish or that bloody mob, we shall not be moved'.

Eventually found a carriage that wasn't full. Sweat pouring off us, wasn't easy carrying a crate of beer, each, 24 cans in a crate. Hoped that would see us through to (pauses) Carlisle at least!

Only one occupant, man with his face buried in a paper. Put the crates in the overhead, took off my jacket, tammy and scarf, Christ they trains were like ovens. Collapsed onto the seats, exhausted. Jack turned up his radio, loved his music.

TAM
Turn that pish off.

Tam walks over to Jack, takes his radio, opens the window, chucks it out.

JACK
A simple, 'can you turn that pish down', I would have got the hint. Know how much that cost?

TAM
Only a radio son, not as if I cut off your ears. I could cut off your ears if you'd like me to. (he brings out a kitchen knife)

JACK
No, you're ok, quite attached to my ears.

JIMMY
(to Tam) And they're quite attached to him!

TAM
Good lad. (putting the knife away) We've got a long night ahead of us so we can do this the hard way or my way, your call.

OLD JIMMY (NARRATING)
Sat in silence, shiting it to say a thing. Even the noise of the ring pull when we opened a can sounded

like an explosion. Then about ten minutes later things picked up when this lassie entered the carriage.

JACK
(to Georgy) How do you do, I'm Jack.

GEORGY
Hi, I'm Georgy.

JACK
So, are you off to the London?

GEORGY
Aye, I've got a photo shoot, I'm a model. Well part time model.

JACK
A model!

GEORGY
Like your hair.

JACK
What, eh, oh, aye?

GEORGY
No split ends.

JACK
Like to take care of my hair.

JIMMY
Poster boy for Sunsilk, him!

JACK
Been told I look a bit like Georgie Best in a certain light.

JIMMY
A broken light.

TAM
(to Jack) Georgie Worst more like, did you choose that hair-style son or was it a bet?

JACK
Nothing wrong with it.

TAM
Seen less grease in a chip-pan.

GEORGY
I think it's with it. I work in that new unisex salon in Shawlands.

JACK
Uni_sex_!

GEORGY
We cut women _and_ men's hair.

TAM
Know the kind of men go into that type of place.

GEORGY
What kind?

TAM
You know the ones I mean hen, the umbrella carriers.

GEORGY
Umbrellas!

TAM
Them that are a bit 'light on their feet'.

JIMMY
They're going to make that legal.

GEORGY
Carrying umbrellas?

JIMMY
No.

TAM
Way things are going in this country they'll be making it compulsory!

GEORGY
You've lost me!

TAM
Bum bandits, poofs, fairies, queers, queens.

GEORGY
Oh, the gays, I thought you were talking about footballers.

TAM
_No_ footballers are gay hen.

GEORGY

Always hugging and kissing, in the bath, in the scud! Is that not a bit...?

TAM

Horseplay.

GEORGY

That what you call it, all they men in the buff, together!

TAM

These are football players.

GEORGY

Loads of footballers must be gay. Tons of actors are (pauses) Rock Hudson for instance.

TAM:

Big Rock, no way, he shagged Doris Day.

GEORGY

Raymond Burr.

TAM

Perry Mason? Perry's not a fairy.

GEORGY

So, must be loads of footballers that are gay.

TAM

Utter nonsense, there are none. Name me one, just one, go on? (pauses) See, you can't.

GEORGY

I don't know many football players (thinks) eh, what about him plays for England (pauses) the captain with the blonde curly hair?

TAM

Bobby Moore! (thinks for a bit) Oh aye, now I come to think about it, he's as camp as the Christmas lights in George Square!

OLD JIMMY (NARRATING)

Thing is, she was right, must have been loads of footballers that were gay but how many would admit it? None! Must be even more now but how many would admit it in these new enlightened times?

Aye, none! Some things haven't progressed that much in 50 years!

Then, there were the years of 'we hate Jimmy Hill, he's a poof, he's a poof'. Didn't hate Jimmy Hill because of his sexual orientation or even because he was English, hated him because he was a dick! But if you were a homosexual Scotland fan, and there must have been loads, how would that song make you feel? 'We hate Jimmy Hill, he's a Jew', get the jail for that. 'He's a poof', bit of banter, eh.

These were the days before we sang 'Bobby Moore, superstar, walks like a woman and he wears a bra'. Deep down we knew that wasn't true, was never a superstar!

JIMMY
Live and let live, that's my motto. About time they made it legal. Nobody else's business if a guy fancies a guy. What harm does it do to anyone?

TAM
You a shirt lifter?

JIMMY
I'm getting married!

TAM
Most homosexuals are married sunshine, well known fact. It's un-natural, it's in the bible, Adam and Eve, <u>Adam and Eve</u>, not Adam and (pauses) bloody Steve!

JIMMY
Talk shite! Your palming off dirty books where guys are having it away with cows, bloody hypocrite.

JACK
Jimmy!

TAM
Cheeky wee shite, touched a nerve have I?

GEORGY
Get loads of footballers in the salon. Tommy Gemmell has been in, bit dry but lots of body (pauses) his hair that is! (laughs in a very distinctive manner which she repeats throughout the play) Ronnie McKinnon, what a honey. Dresses like a film star. (to Jimmy) That's a lovely suit you're wearing.

JIMMY
Suit maketh the man, not like baw-face here, (nodding at Jack) makes Albert Steptoe look like James Bond.

(in Sean Connery accent) '<u>Jack</u> Wilshon, lishenshed to look like a tosher'!

JACK
(to Georgy also in a Sean Connery accent) Sho shweetheart, fanshy the shinema shometime shoon?

GEORGY
Love the pictures. Sound of Music is back on, seen it ten times, all they songs are smashing, Climb Every Mountain, My Favourite Things, Do-a deer..

JIMMY
No, not Do-a deer, he'll never stop...

JACK
...a deer, a female deer. (Do-Re-Mi has been a favourite song with Scotland fans for the past 20 years so the audience might join in)

JIMMY
Shut up!

GEORGY
(to Jimmy) Do you not like the songs from The Sound of Music?

JIMMY
Just the one about him. (nods at Jack)

GEORGY
Which one is that?

JIMMY
Idle swine!

GEORGY
(laughs) Films, music, fashion, it's all happening in London. I'm hoping to be Glasgow's answer to Twiggy.

TAM
If you're the answer hen, Christ knows what the question was! If you don't mind me saying dear, are you not a wee bit, eh, on the heavy side to be the next Twiggy? 'Loggy', might be a better name?

JACK
(to Georgy) Never mind him, I think you look smashing, like my woman with a bit of meat.

JIMMY
Usually just have chips with my meat!

JACK
A woman should look like a woman, not a wee boy like that Twiggy.

GEORGY
Got a girlfriend?

JACK
Interested?

GEORGY
(laughs) As if! So where are you boys off to?

JACK
The match.

GEORGY
Who's playing?

JACK
Scotland! Scotland, England, biggest match in the world.

JIMMY
Been going to Wembley for years. But this one, this is the biggest one ever, well after last summer.

GEORGY
Last summer?

JIMMY
That mob won the World Cup.

GEORGY
Which mob?

JACK
England, f'n England.

GEORGY
Did they?

JIMMY
Christ hen, you just back from the moon?

GEORGY
So, England is the best team in the world then?

JIMMY
Bloody cheated.

JACK
In the final, scored a goal that wasn't a goal.

JIMMY
Lines-man gave it but it wasn't.

GEORGY
Wasn't what?

JACK
A goal, the whole f'n ball has to cross the line.
(makes circling gesture a few times and Jimmy does likewise)

JIMMY
So, that's how 'that mob' won...

JACK
Stole...

JIMMY
...stole the World Cup.

OLD JIMMY (NARRATING)
Wait until I show you this.

VFX:	England's third 'goal' – ON

OLD JIMMY (NARRATING)
What do you think, did it cross the line? Remember the whole ball has to cross the line. (makes circling gesture a few times) You must have seen it a million times, I mean it's been shown more often than that Kennedy bloke getting shot. Never mind your grassy knoll and magic bullet conspiracies' shite, who bribed that bloody Russian linesman, there's the story of the 60s?

VFX:	England's third 'goal' – OFF

JIMMY
Punter ran on the pitch.

JACK
Against the rules.

JIMMY
Should have been a 'stoat up'.

JACK
That's why this is the biggest Wembley ever.

GEORGY

Because England won the world cup?

JIMMY

No, they didn't win it! How many times do I need to explain this, they didn't win the World Cup, they stole it, stole the f'n thing!

OLD JIMMY (NARRATING)

I mean what do you think, did they win or did they steal it? (pause for reaction) I mean if we had qualified, we would have won it. Look at the players we had, (counting the players with his fingers) Law, Baxter, Jimmy Johnstone, Henderson, Greig, McNeil, Mackay...

TAM

...hard, hard bastard!

OLD JIMMY (NARRATING)

...St. John, Cooke, Gemmell, McKinnon, Gilzean and the rest. (then counting the 'ifs' on his fingers) If they had played it in Scotland, if they had let us play every game at Hampden, if we were given an easy draw.

Ok, I admit that's quite a lot of 'ifs' but, as the old saying goes, if my aunty had balls, she'd be my uncle but that's not the point because my auntie doesn't have balls and she's not my uncle, do you see where I'm coming from?

JIMMY

We're out to avenge a terrible wrong done to our German cousins.

JACK

Ich bin ein Berliner!

JIMMY

Well said, Adolf.

GEORGY

You like Germany better than England? After fighting them in two world wars! This is a daft wee football match.

JACK

Daft wee football match, listen to Twiggy!

GEORGY

Bet that's all you think about, football (pauses) and sex. That's all Glasgow men think about, football and sex.

JACK
I'm not having that, I know some Glasgow men that don't think about sex!

TAM
Tell you what hen, if the 'Glasgow Twiggy' thing doesn't work out and you're looking for a job in the Big Smoke, here (hands Georgy a card). Pop in and we'll see how you measure up. Any experience?

GEORGY
Gentlemen's club!

JACK
Need to get your thrupney bits out!

TAM
£2 a night, cash in hand. Just a wee shoogle about in your vest and pants, very tasteful.

Georgy hands back the card.

GEORGY
You're ok.

JIMMY
Could you get him a job?

JACK
Don't have thrupney bits!

TAM
Just so happens I have a vacancy, one of my door-men had a tragic accident. Mind you he doesn't know it yet! (laughs)

JIMMY
(to Jack) There you go Pisces boy, working at a strip club, your dream job, no need to think too long about that!

JACK
What would I do?

TAM
Hang around the entrance, get the punters to come in.

JACK
How would I do that?

                    TAM
It's not that complicated sunshine, just shout something like, 'they are naked and they move'.

                    JACK
(practising) They are naked and they move. They are naked and they move. They are...

                    JIMMY
He's a natural, when can he start?

                    TAM
Bit on the weedy side, need someone who can handle themselves.

                    JIMMY
Not had a woman for ages, he's had loads of practice handling himself!

                    JACK
They are naked and they move.

                    OLD JIMMY (NARRATING)
The train slowed down. The big man looked out the window.

                    JACK
Where are we?

                    TAM
Crewe.

                    JACK
Where's Crewe?

                    JIMMY
Near the top of the fourth division, boom, boom, the old ones are the best!

                    OLD JIMMY (NARRATING)
The big man looked agitated, quickly gathered up his belongings.

                    TAM
Can't sit here all day listening to your shite.

Tam hurriedly leaves.

                    JIMMY
Thank Christ he's away, gave me the creeps.

Jack starts to impersonate Tam.

JACK
What was he like, never trouble, trouble until trouble troubles you, what a big fanny!

GEORGY
Right, I'll need to leave you as well.

JACK
No, we're just getting to know each other.

GEORGY
Think I know you well enough.

JACK
Come on, you can't leave me with him. (nodding at Jimmy)

JIMMY
Thanks pal.

GEORGY
Really need to go, nice meeting you both, might see you again some time.

JACK
We'll be in the Station cafe until the pubs open at lunchtime if you fancy it. Just round the corner from Euston.

GEORGY
(distracted) Aye, aye, whatever, I'll need to run.

Georgy leaves

JIMMY
Well, just the two of us, bit of peace and quiet, might get a kip now.

JACK
Think I'm in love. (impersonates Georgy) 'Glasgow's answer to Twiggy'.

JIMMY
Aye, she was nice, just glad that big nut job is away.

JACK
(impersonates Tam) Never trouble, trouble until trouble troubles you. Never trouble, trouble until trouble troubles you.

Tam has returned and standing at the door, Jack can't see him.

JACK
Never trouble, trouble until trouble troubles you. Never trouble, trouble until trouble troubles you, big fanny!

Tam coughs.

JACK
What the f! Eh look, eh sorry Mr Tunnock, just a bit of fun.

TAM
Lucky I have a sense of humour, well known for it. Was wondering if you lads could do me a wee favour?

JACK
What?

TAM
Could you hang onto this bag for a few hours? (giving Jack a card) Deliver it to that address, that's my club. Be there at 7:00 tonight.

JACK
What's in it for us?

TAM
Make it worth your while, don't let it out of your sight and whatever you do, <u>don't</u> open it."

JIMMY
Eh, I'm not sure about...

JACK
£20.

TAM
£20!

JACK
Each.

TAM
Do you know who you're dealing with <u>little man</u>?

JACK
Sorry (pauses) Mister Tunnock make it £30 (pauses) each.

TAM
You're pushing it little man.

JACK
Did I say £30, sorry, I meant £40 (pauses) each. We can do this the hard way or my way sunshine! (in a sing song voice) Never trouble trouble until trouble troubles you!

OLD JIMMY (NARRATING)
There was an announcement, the train was departing in one minute.

TAM:
(to Jimmy) Do you trust him?

JIMMY
With my life (pauses) but not with my wallet!

TAM
(counts out the money) (to Jack) £80, here. 7:00 on the dot. It's opening night and I have a ton of important people coming and I'll need that bag so don't be late or I will rip out your intestines, hang you from a tree then force you to listen to Calum Kennedy.

Tam leaves.

JACK
£80! Dancer.

JIMMY
Shouldn't get mixed up with nutters like him.

JACK
Easy money.

JIMMY
Right, kip time. At least we've now got space for a lie down.

Jack takes off his scarf to make a pillow. Jimmy goes to pick up his scarf but it's missing.

JIMMY
Seen my scarf?

JACK
What?

JIMMY

My scarf, my lucky scarf.

JACK

Have you checked the overhead?

JIMMY

Of course, I've checked it, stop fannying about and give me my scarf. You know how much that scarf means to me. If I don't find it we're as well not going on Saturday. Where is it?

JACK

Don't have it, swear to God. Maybe nut-job or Twiggy took it?

JIMMY

Don't be daft. What would they want with my scarf?

JACK

Got £80, we can get tons of scarves.

JIMMY

That was my lucky scarf, what chance do we have now?

OLD JIMMY (NARRATING)

Once again Jack had put us in the shit, getting involved with that big nut-job. It would end in tears, it always did!

LX:	**Lights down**

VFX:	**Georgy Girl by The Seekers**

ACT 1 SCENE 4 – CAFÉ, LONDON (14 APRIL 1967, 11:00)

LX:	Centre stage

Jimmy and Jack are sitting at a table reading newspapers.

OLD JIMMY (NARRATING)
In the morning, we get to Euston, headed straight to left luggage, no way we'd be wandering about the London with that bag. After depositing the bag, we headed to the Station Cafe, fry up time. We were Hank Marvin, cream crackered, hadn't got much sleep, train was like an oven.

JIMMY
English papers, every one of them, going to get our arses felt.

JACK
What do they know?

JIMMY
Bookies as well.

JACK
Aye, we're four to one. A Scotland team with Law, Baxter, Bremner and the rest, four to one! And nine to four Denis to score anytime, Denis scores against them every time. Not even a bet, it's a donation from the bookies.

JIMMY
Aye well, you said you weren't going to gamble this week-end. Just as well you're skint.

JACK
But four to one Scotland and nine to four the Lawman, sweeties from a wean that is.

OLD JIMMY (NARRATING)
Ding, dong, this glamorous women entered the cafe, mini-skirt, thigh high boots. Looked like a film star.

JACK
Get a load of that!

JIMMY
Shut it.

JACK
(shouting to the woman) All right doll?

GEORGY
If it's not Bonnie and Clyde!

JACK
Do we know you hen?

GEORGY
You boys going to the biggest Wembley ever (laughs and takes off her dark glasses)?

JIMMY
If it's not the Glasgow Twiggy!

JACK
Like the gear.

GEORGY
So how are Bonnie and Clyde?

JACK
What?

GEORGY
Surprised you've not been lifted yet?

JACK
What?

GEORGY
Police are after you two, they're all over the station.

JIMMY
On about?

GEORGY
A murder on the train, just past Crewe. Stabbed twenty times, body dumped on the train track.

JACK
That got to do with us?

GEORGY
There was a tartan scarf beside the body.

JACK
That got to do with us, thousands of tartan scarves?

GEORGY
Not with someone's name and address sewn into it.

JACK
(laughs) Who'd do such a daft thing?

JIMMY
My lucky tartan scarf, you dancer.

JACK
You sewed your name and address, on a scarf?

JIMMY
Aye, well Annie sewed it. You dancer.

GEORGY
Think you might be missing the more important point.

JIMMY
More important than finding my lucky tartan scarf?

GEORGY
Police think the two of you murdered someone.

JIMMY
Don't be daft, nobody could think that we would murder anyone.

GEORGY
Well, the victim was English, was wearing a Union Jack waistcoat. Two of you had quite a bit to drink. Your attitude towards the English is not that friendly, English bastards was that what you called them?

JIMMY
Bit of banter, we don't actually hate the English.

GEORGY
Means, motive, opportunity.

JACK
Sound like a cop! Don't be daft, who'd think we'd be murderers, couple of ordinary working men from Glasgow?

JIMMY
One ordinary working man and one ordinary lazy bastard! Anyway, my lucky tartan scarf, did they say where it is? Had it since I binned my old one after the 9-3 game. My lucky tartan scarf, undefeated at Wembley, need to get it back before the game.

Georgy laughs.

JACK

She's winding us up, very funny Twiggy.

GEORGY

Was on the 10:00 news this morning.

JACK

Rubbish.

GEORGY

Gave out your names and where you stay, Gorbals, aye?

JACK

Eh, aye.

GEORGY

Gave descriptions, one good looking, short ginger hair, smartly dressed, the other, baw-face, greasy hair, dressed like a tramp.

JIMMY

Uncanny!

JACK

Wind up merchant.

OLD JIMMY (NARRATING)

So, she turned on her radio, we heard the last part of the 11:00 news (in a posh accent) a baw-face, greasy hair and dressed like a tramp. In other news'.

Georgy switches off the radio.

GEORGY

There you go.

JACK

(to Jimmy) Do I have a baw-face?

JIMMY

Never mind your baw-face, what about my lucky scarf!

JACK

I don't have a baw-face.

GEORGY

Go to the police, you've nothing to hide.

JACK

Aye, well.

JIMMY

Do you think they'll have my scarf?

                    GEORGY
Aye well, what?

                    JACK
That big nut-job gave us a bag to deliver, to his club tonight, if we don't do it not very nice things are going to happen to us.

                    GEORGY
Like what?

                    JIMMY
Calum Kennedy is involved, let's just leave it at that!

Jack makes a shivering noise.

                    GEORGY
What's in the bag?

                    JIMMY
We don't know.

                    JACK
I know.

                    JIMMY
What?

                    JACK
Well it's not sweeties.

                    GEORGY
Where is it?

                    JIMMY
Left luggage.

                    JACK
You ask a lot of questions for a model!

                    GEORGY
Just trying to help. Do you know what kind of drugs they are?

                    JIMMY
There are drugs in the bag?

                    JACK

Told you it wasn't sweeties. Eh, (to Georgy) how did you know there were drugs in the bag?

GEORGY
You said it wasn't sweeties, what else could it be? Go to the police, turn yourselves in.

JIMMY
Police think we're murderers, might lock us up.

JACK
We could miss the match.

JIMMY
Aye, we could miss the match, Christ that's all we need, biggest Wembley ever.

GEORGY
Don't start that again. Look, turn yourselves in, take the bag to the police, it will be fine.

JACK
And what if we miss the match, don't think so hen.

JIMMY
We could go to the police after the match?

JACK
Now there's a plan. How are we going to get out of the station?

GEORGY
What else is in the bag?

JACK
About four grand.

JIMMY
What?

GEORGY
What if you give me the bag, I'll take it to the police and explain the situation? There is a reward, we could split it three ways?

JACK
Now there's a better plan!

JIMMY
Don't know. You seem awfully interested in (sarcastically) helping us. What's in it for you.

GEORGY

What are you insinuating?

JIMMY

For all we know, you and Tunnock are joined at the hip and are setting us up.

GEORGY

You've been watching too many James Bond movies.

JIMMY

Don't know, something seems a bit odd.

GEORGY

Keep your stupid bag then, just trying to help (wipes away a tear).

JACK

(to Jimmy) Now look what you've done. (puts his arm around Georgy and broadly smiles at Jimmy) There, there, pet, just ignore him.

GEORGY

Well, if you don't want my help, I've got places to go.

JACK

And leave us here? Where are you off to?

GEORGY

Test shoot, Subway Model Agency.

JACK

<u>Models</u>!

JIMMY

Well we've got White Hart Lane, Stamford Bridge and ...

GEORGY

You'll do well to get out the station (pointing), police are everywhere.

JACK

(to Georgy) Can we come with you, please, pretty please?

GEORGY

If you want, but you'll need to figure out how to get past those police.

JACK

What are we going to do?

JIMMY
This is all your fault, Christ, might miss the match, lucky tartan scarf lost...

JACK
...it's not really lost...

GEORGY
Don't forget wanted for murder.

JIMMY
(nonchalantly) Aye, that as well, but my <u>lucky tartan scarf</u>!

JACK
What are we going to do about the police?

GEORGY
If the police stop us, I'm not with you, right?

JIMMY
(to Georgy) What's in the suitcase?

GEORGY
Modelling outfits for the photo shoot.

JACK
So, these models. (rubs his hands) Are they naked and they move?

JIMMY
Here's an idea.

OLD JIMMY (NARRATING)
Well, we didn't want to take the chance of missing the biggest Wembley ever.

| **LX** | **Lights down** |

| **VFX** | **Music to Watch Girls by Andy Williams** |

ACT 1 SCENE 5 - PHOTO STUDIO, LONDON (15:00)

LX	Centre stage

OLD JIMMY (NARRATING)
We'd been sitting in this photo studio for two hours, two f'n hours, waiting for Georgy's name to be called. Really hacked off,

I had been looking forward to going around the football grounds and we were sitting on our arses doing hee haw. But Jack, kid in a sweetie shop. Models, models, more models, absolutely stunning. The Locarno was never like this!

He was giving it 'how is it going doll' every time a new model came in but they all 'dingied' him. Oh, did I mention, we were dressed as women!

Jimmy and Jack are in drag and attempt to talk like women when talking to strangers.

JIMMY
This is a waste of time.

JACK
Waste of time! Get a grip, look at these models. (whistles) How is it going doll?

JIMMY
Behave yourself.

JACK
Never seen so many beautiful women, I'm not going anywhere.

GEORGY
I've got no chance with this competition.

JACK
Rubbish, you're just as beautiful as any of them.

OLD JIMMY (NARRATING)
So, Terence, the photographer, appeared. Know the type, full of themselves, think they're God's gift. Loads of impressionable wee lassies that would do anything to make it as a model. He would take full advantage.

TERENCE
(shouting) Georgy, Georgy McAlister?

GEORGY
That's me.

JIMMY
At last.

TERENCE
How do you do, pleasure to make your acquaintance. Sorry to have kept you waiting so long, been absolutely insane today darling. Wow, you are absolutely gorgeous.

GEORGY
Thanks.

TERENCE
Not you silly, (looking at Jack) this little bundle of sex.

GEORGY
What! Eh, eh...

TERENCE
What's your name sexy?

JACK
Jack, eh aline, Jacqueline, pleased to meet you.

TERENCE
You are gor-ge-ous.

GEORGY
What!

TERENCE
You must have done some modelling?

GEORGY
Aye, Airfix.

TERENCE
You have such a unique look.

JACK
Unique?

GEORGY
Means ugly.

TERENCE
Nothing of the sort. There is a unique symmetry to your face.

Jack looks confused.

GEORGY
He means you've got a baw-face Jacqueline!

TERENCE
Boffice?

OLD JIMMY (NARRATING)
She had to explain to the bold Terence that a baw-face was a face shaped like a ball, (makes circling gesture), you know like the whole bloody ball needs to cross the line! He understood (snaps fingers) like that, if only that bloody Russian linesman was as quick on the uptake!

TERENCE
Yes, yes, you're absolutely correct, she has a face like a ball, the ball-face woman, this could be huge. Here come with me.

JACK
What!

OLD JIMMY (NARRATING)
Terence took Jack by the hand and they went into the next room.

JIMMY
What was that all about? Will he be ok?

GEORGY
As if the competition isn't hard enough even your ugly pal is ahead of me!

JIMMY
He's not seriously going to photograph him, is he?

OLD JIMMY (NARRATING)
Couldn't understand why this guy was so interested in Jack, he was no oil painting even with the make-up on but then I thought about Twiggy. Who would have thought that a skinny wee lassie would become a world famous model? Ugly, baw-faced men, sorry women, might be the next big thing! Everything was changing so fast back then, nothing would have surprised you. So, Jack came out.

JACK
(to Jimmy) Come through, he wants us to get changed, just the two of us?

46.

GEORGY

(to Terence) Look you, what's the score? Been waiting here for ages and you're going to photograph that ugly baw-faced idiot and his, eh her, pal? You're not on.

TERENCE

Well darling, it's like, eh, look, I need to (pauses) I've an idea. I really want to photograph the ball-face woman so why doesn't she and her friend...(points at Jimmy)

JIMMY

Jimmy...mima, Jemima.

TERENCE

...Jemima, pop next door to the wardrobe room, pick out something sexy and I'll do the two of you? Come on I don't have all day.

Jimmy and Jack go into the room.

OLD JIMMY (NARRATING)

Terence ushered Jack and me into the next room while he stayed with Georgy who kept moaning at him.

TERENCE

Can I ask you darling, are your two friends, party girls?

GEORGY

What?

TERENCE

You know (winks) do they like to party.

GEORGY

Oh, aye, eh, no, I'm not sure.

TERENCE

That Jacqueline, she looks like she's been around the block a few times.

GEORGY

Oh, to party, now I get you. Oh, aye, can't get enough of the partying those two.

TERENCE

Do you think Jacqueline would fancy going to a party later? I have a friend who would just love to get it on with her, he has a major thing for Scots girls.

47.

                    GEORGY
Oh, aye, definitely.

                    TERENCE
Fab new strip joint, totally happening. Tonight's the
grand opening.

                    GEORGY
I'll ask baw-face. (shouting through the wall) Do you
fancy a party later?

                    JIMMY
No.

                    JACK
Aye.

                    JIMMY
No.

                    GEORGY
Nobody's asking you.

                    JIMMY
Who?

                    JACK
Who?

                    GEORGY
You! Baw-face, do you want to go to a party tonight.

                    JACK
You dancer. Absolutely doll. Knew you couldn't resist
my animal magnetism.

                    GEORGY
As if.

                    JACK
Will there be booze?

Georgy looks at Terence who nods.

                    GEORGY
Aye.

                    JACK
What about Jimmy...

                    JIMMY

...Jemima.

JACK
Aye, is he, eh she going as well?

GEORGY
No.

JACK
Why not?

JIMMY
Why am I not going?

Georgy looks at Terence who makes a 'possible' gesture.

GEORGY
Depends if you're a party girl?

JIMMY
I'm a party girl alright. We're both party girls.

Terence gives an enthusiastic double thumbs-up.

GEORGY
Ok, you're in. Get a move on (looks at her watch) Women eh, ages to get ready!

TERENCE
Excellent. My friend will just love those husky Scots voices. Here's the name and address of the club. (hands Georgy a piece of paper) He and I have many shared business interests if you know what I mean. (taps his nose)

GEORGY
(inspecting the paper) TCs.

TERENCE
Tell the doorman that Terence sent you and he'll introduce you to my friend.

JACK
Be out in a minute, Christ these hot pants are tight. How are you coping Jimmy...mima?

JIMMY
Just about there, here we go.

OLD JIMMY (NARRATING)
I was first out, yellow flowery blouse, yellow hot pants, sunglasses and a floppy yellow hat. Terence

looked pleased. Jack came out wearing identical gear. Terence gave him a hug and a pat on the backside.

TERENCE
Just like twins, scrumptious!

GEORGY
If it's not the Glasgow Kinks, dedicated followers of shite!

TERENCE
Jacqueline, could you come with me? I'll give you a shout in ten minutes Jemima, (pauses) better make that fifteen and I'll then do the two of you.

JIMMY
'Do the two of us', that's the second time he's said that, what does he mean!

GEORGY
Bloody baw-face!

OLD JIMMY (NARRATING)
So off they went to the next room, Terence with his around Jack's waist. Heard the door getting locked, thought that was odd.

JIMMY
Will he be all right?

GEORGY
What could possibly happen with baw-face?

OLD JIMMY (NARRATING)
So, a minute later there is this almighty thud and out runs Jack.

JACK
Quick, up the road, run.

OLD JIMMY (NARRATING)
So, we all just ran. Out the studio, down the street, jumped on the first bus we saw.

JIMMY
What was all that about?

JACK
Bloody pervert!

JIMMY
Who?

JACK
Your man, Terence, tried to touch me.

JIMMY
Where?

JACK
In that studio.

JIMMY
No, I mean where did he try to touch you?

JACK
Everywhere.

JIMMY
Where?

JACK
(pointing) There, there and there.

JIMMY
There!

JACK
Aye, especially there!

JIMMY
But there's nothing there .

JACK
Aye, but that didn't stop him! Was like a bloody Octopus! Men!

GEORGY
Sure you weren't leading him on?

JACK
I'm not that kind of girl. Then he asked if I'd take my clothes off.

GEORGY
What, a wee shoogle about in your vest and pants, very tasteful?

JACK
So, I belted him and got off my mark.

GEORGY
They are naked and they move!

                              JACK
　　That's not funny.

                             GEORGY
　　Aye it is!

LX	Lights down

VFX	I Second That Emotion by Smokey Robinson

ACT 2 SCENE 1 – NIGHT CLUB, LONDON (20:00)

VFX:	Incense and Peppermint by Strawberry Alarm Clock

LX	Centre stage

OLD JIMMY (NARRATING)

So, we had a choice to make for our night-time festivities. Option one, we get out of these bloody women's clothes, get the bag, deliver it to the big man's club and Jack gets to see the naked women but the downside, a huge, bloody big downside, we might get arrested and miss the match. Option 2, we keep wearing these bloody women's clothes, don't get the bag, don't deliver it to the big man's club, go to a different club, Jack still gets to see naked women and we both get to see the match. No brainer as they say nowadays. Pass the lipstick!

GEORGY

TCs, here we are.

JACK

'TCs', that sounds familiar.

OLD JIMMY (NARRATING)

So, we're at the bar, it's dark apart from psychedelic lights shining on the walls and there's music, really loud.

GEORGY

Right, now that you're women for the night, two rules. One, the two of you stick together, don't go anywhere on your own.

JACK

What about the bogs?

GEORGY

Especially the toilets.

JACK

So that's why they do that, it's a rule!

GEORGY

Two, keep your drinks with you all the time.

JACK

Not a problem, always do, why's that a problem?

GEORGY

In case some nut job slips something into it.

53.

                          JACK
You don't need to treat us like we boys.

                          JIMMY
Wee lassies!

                          JACK
Like wee lassies.

                          GEORGY
Just stick to the rules.

                   OLD JIMMY (NARRATING)
Already had a few scoops so we were a bit unsteady on
our feet, the high heels didn't help! I got the
bevvys in.

Having had a few, the guys Glasgow accents are a bit stronger
than usual!

                          JIMMY
(to the barman who has blonde hair) Whoa blondey,
Bobby Moore, two pints of Tennents and a Martini.

                          BARMAN
What was that darling?

                          JIMMY
(shouting) Two pints of Tennents and a Martini.

                          BARMAN
Sorry dear, do you speak English?

                          JACK
Here, I'll deal with this, I know how to talk to
these people. (shouting louder) Tennents. (making a
'T' sign with his fingers) Two. (holds up two
fingers). Get that sunshine? And a Martini.

                          BARMAN
Come again.

                          JIMMY
Ok, two whiskeys then. And a Martini.

                          BARMAN
Here you go ladies, 5 shillings.

                          JIMMY
5 shillings, said two whiskies not twenty two! Be a
short night at these prices.

BARMAN
And what are you lovely Scots girls up to?

JIMMY
Down for the game, Scotland, England, biggest Wembley ever.

BARMAN
Ladies who like football! How do you think the match will go?

JACK
Sweeties from a wean.

BARMAN
Sorry.

JACK
Sorry on the other side of your face ramorra.

BARMAN
My face?

JIMMY
None of you speak English down here?

JACK
Have your heed in your hands to play with son.

BARMAN
Your heed?

JACK
Aye, getting pumped.

BARMAN
Pumped?

JACK
Erses well and truly felt.

BARMAN
Erses?

JACK
(grabbing his own backside to demonstrate) Erse, well and truly felt.

BARMAN
Would you be looking to score?

JIMMY

Course we're bloody looking to score, think that we'd have travelled over 400 miles if we weren't looking to score. Got the 'Law-man' on our side, we'll score alright, no danger.

GEORGY

What do you make of this place?

JACK

It's not The Plaza!

JIMMY

Five bob for two whiskies and a Martini...

JACK

...that tastes like pish. Hope some of they models come.

GEORGY

And what would you do if they did <u>Jacqueline</u>, dressed like a woman?

JACK

Let's get a good table beside the stage, don't want to miss a thing. They are naked and they're about to move!

OLD JIMMY (NARRATING)

And as we were about to make our way over to a table, the doorman told us that the owner would like to see us in the VIP lounge.

JACK

Ya dancer.

OLD JIMMY (NARRATING)

So, we get escorted in, through the silver curtains, feeling like films stars, this is going to be good. A man is sitting in the room with his face buried in a paper. The paper came down, Tam!

TAM

Evening ladies. Couldn't help noticing you were on your lonesome. You're all looking lovely. Park your backsides over here. I'm Thomas by the way, welcome to my club. And you are?

JACK

Jack...eline.

JIMMY

Jemima.

GEORGY

Barbara.

TAM

Can I get you girls a drink?

JACK

Eh, aye, aye. Two pints of Tenn...

JIMMY

...eh Martinis.

TAM

Two pints of Martinis!

JIMMY

Sorry make that three.

TAM

Everyone likes a girl that likes a drink! Think we're going to have a good time, the four of us. Can you excuse me for a few minutes, some business I need to attend to? Back in a tick.

OLD JIMMY (NARRATING)

So, as he leaves, he gives me a peck on the cheek! And me engaged as well!

JACK

VIP lounge, this is brilliant.

JIMMY

You didn't know this was Tea-cake's club?

JACK

How would I know?

JIMMY

He gave you his card!

JACK

Oh, aye. 'TCs', that's where I'd seen it. Aye.

JIMMY

You didn't think it might be worth mentioning before we came in?

JACK

VIP lounge, turned out fine.

JIMMY
Need to get out of here. We don't have his bag. He thinks that we're women and looks like he fancies me!

JACK
He could do worse, you've scrubbed up not bad. Like a younger, sexier version of your old dear.

JIMMY
Cheers!

JACK
Must fancy his chances.

JIMMY
I'm not that kind of girl.

JACK
Neither am I but it didn't stop that chancer at the photo studio.

GEORGY
That's men for you, anything in a skirt.

JACK
And a pulse, some of us are more choosy!

GEORGY
Baw-face this afternoon, (to Jimmy) now you. I might as well chuck it.

JACK
I could have been Glasgow's answer to Twiggy!

GEORGY
Shut it.

JACK
Just kidding, you're gorgeous.

GEORGY
Cheers Jacqueline!

Tam returns.

OLD JIMMY (NARRATING)
We didn't say anything, shiting it. Fluttered my eyelashes and Jack did the same, men love that! See this 'being a woman' stuff, piece of cake.

TAM
Cat got your tongue ladies?

                    JIMMY
Eh, I just need to pop to the little girl's room.

                    GEORGY
Rule number one.

                    JACK
Oh, aye, me as well, where's my purse?

                    TAM
Ok, well hurry back.

            OLD JIMMY (NARRATING)
Off we went to the bogs. So, we're in the women's toilets, aye! Ever been in the women's toilets, well of course you have if you're a woman but if you're not a woman! Christ, they can talk! I'm sitting in a cubicle minding my own business and the woman in the next cubicle strikes up a conversation. In the toilet, what's that all about! It's hard enough concentrating on the job in hand without getting the third degree. So back we went the VIP lounge.

                    TAM
Don't recognise you girls and I know all the Glasgow scrubbers on the London circuit.

                    GEORGY
Not on the circuit and we're not scrubbers.

                    TAM
Loads of money on the stripper circuit hen, wee honeys like you three, would clean up. Not to be sniffed at. How long have you been in the London?

                    JACK
Just arrived, down on the sleeper last night.

                    JIMMY
Jack...aline!

                    JACK
What?

                    TAM
There's a coincidence, I was on that train as well.

                    JIMMY
Aye, small world.

                    TAM

Too small a world, had a bit of bother, cops all over the shop, had to give some merchandise to a couple of wee fannies coming down for the game, meeting them here tonight.

JIMMY
Oh aye.

TAM
Cops were closing in, thing is, don't know how they knew I was on that train, thought I'd covered my tracks, must have been followed. Gave the wee fannies £80 but I'll take it back as soon as they show up and break their f'n legs for their f'n cheek, teach the wee fannies a lesson, taking liberties with me.

JACK
Aye, teach the wee fannies a lesson, quite right!

JIMMY
Liberty takers!

TAM
And they're late. Wouldn't like to be in their shoes when they do show up, not that they'll need shoes after I've finished with them! (laughs) Don't need shoes if you've no legs eh?(laughs)

JIMMY
Aye!

TAM
Should have been here ages ago. Excuse me a second (picks up phone) Hello, any sign of those wee shites? (pauses) Ok, give me a bell as soon as they get here.

GEORGY
No joy?

TAM
Wee fannies still not here.

JIMMY
The wee fannies!

GEORGY
I'll need to pop to the little girls room.

JIMMY
(to Jack) Rule number one.

JACK

Oh aye, we'll come with you.

GEORGY
It's ok (pauses), I need to call my mother as well, let her know what I'm up to. It's fine.

Georgy leaves.

TAM
So, girls, would you like something with your drinks?

OLD JIMMY (NARRATING)
We thought he meant like a packet of smoky bacon or salted peanuts but he had a plastic bag full of Smarties, well they looked like Smarties. Smarties with a drink! Thought it must have been a London thing!

JACK
Smarties?

TAM
Aye (pause) Smarties, whatever.

Tam gives each of them a small coloured pill.

TAM
Do you like Smarties ladies?

JACK
Love Smarties, anymore?

TAM
One should be enough (pauses) for now (laughs).

Jimmy and Jack eat their 'Smarties'. Georgy returns.

OLD JIMMY (NARRATING)
A few minutes later Jack's arms started shaking and he had a big, daft grin on his coupon. Kept repeating 'Smarties', 'Smarties'! He was about to go on a 'trip'.

JACK
(laughing/repeatedly shouting) Smarties!

| **VFX:** | **Scotland the Brave (techno version) - ON** |

Jack starts dancing a Highland jig.

GEORGY
What's the score with baw-face?

TAM
Didn't take much to get her going, think we're in for a good night tonight!

Jimmy starts dancing a Highland jig.

JACK
(to Jimmy) Love you Jimmy...ima.

JIMMY
Love you more, Jack...eline.

JACK
No, I love you more, Jemima.

TAM
And I love you both!

VFX: Scotland the Brave (techno version) - OFF

GEORGY
What's got into you two?

JACK
(to Tam) Any more Smarties?

TAM
No bother.

Tam attempts to give Jack a 'Smartie' but Georgy intervenes.

GEORGY
Christ, I leave you for a minute. Think you've had enough Smarties for one night Jacqueline. Time I got you up the road.

JACK
No, haven't seen the strippers yet.

TAM
You like looking at naked women?

JACK
Aye, of course, who doesn't?

TAM
We'll get on just fine.

GEORGY
Right, up the road.

TAM
No rush dear, we're just getting warmed up.

OLD JIMMY (NARRATING)
With the loud music, the psychedelic lights, the booze and the Smarties, my head was spinning. Then I threw up! Seriously threw up.

TAM
What the f!

JIMMY
Not feeling well.

JACK
Can't take his Smarties him, eh her, never could! The Maltesers aye, but not the Smarties.

TAM
Look at this mess.

GEORGY
Right, up the road.

TAM
Hen, can you get rid of sick lassie here and Jacqueline and I will get to know each other a bit better.

JACK
Any more Smarties?

TAM
Plenty hen. Let me just go and check to see if they wee fannies are here.

JACK
Wee fannies, aye. (giggles)

Tam gives Jack a peck on the cheek

TAM
Back in ten minutes. (to Jack) Don't you move gorgeous.

JACK
Ok. Strippers. They are naked and they move.

TAM
Aye, that's right, hen, naked and they move.

Tam leaves.

                              GEORGY
Right quick.

                       OLD JIMMY (NARRATING)
Georgy managed to huckle us out the club despite
Jack's protests, caught a taxi and we were offski.

Tam returns.

                              TAM
Still no sign of they wee fannies, they're dead men.
Ok ladies, where were we? (sees that no one is there)
Ladies? (thinks) They are naked and they move!
(thinks) Wee fannies!

LX:	Lights down

VFX:	Don't Sleep in the Subway by Petula Clark

ACT 2, SCENE 2 – BED & BREAKFAST (15 APRIL 1967, 13:00)

LX:	Centre stage

OLD JIMMY (NARRATING)

Next day, day of the match, biggest Wembley ever. What a night we had, couldn't remember a thing mind!

Looked around, grotty B&B. Felt someone moving beside me. I'm in bed with someone. No! Who? I started to piece together the previous night. TCs, Smarties, Tea-cake wanting to get to know me better! Bloody hell. Too scared to look so just lay there trying to figure out what to do.

JIMMY

What have I done?

GEORGY

At last, wondering when you were going to come to. Give your boyfriend a nudge?

JIMMY

Boyfriend!

GEORGY

Tea-cake.

JIMMY

What have I done?

OLD JIMMY (NARRATING)

Lay there, frozen, too scared to move. Then I thought, couldn't have done anything, not with Tea-cake. That big, homophobic chancer. Then again, maybe he was overcompensating with his ranting on the train. Maybe he was a...!

JIMMY

What have I done? Annie will cut my balls off.

GEORGY

Don't be too hard on yourself, attractive woman like you. Hope you took precautions.

JIMMY

What?

GEORGY

The pill, wonder of modern science, stops the ball getting in the net! (puts up her hand)

                    JIMMY
(thinks) Tea-cake said that!

                    GEORGY
Aye, I know.

                    JIMMY
But he said it in the pub and you weren't in the pub?

                    GEORGY
(flustered) Eh, he said it last night after your, eh, eh, love making.

                    JIMMY
What!

                    GEORGY
Had his wicked way with you then offski. Left you a few quid mind and a box of Milk Tray. Men, eh, all the same!

                    JIMMY
What!

                    GEORGY
Soon as they get what they want, you'll not see them for dust.

                    JIMMY
I'm not like that.

                    GEORGY
(laughs) Only kidding. Who do you think it is?

                OLD JIMMY (NARRATING)
Pulled back the covers a wee bit. Long blonde hair so wasn't The Tea-cake! But who was she?

                    JIMMY
What have I done? Annie will cut my balls cut off.

                OLD JIMMY (NARRATING)
There was this loud noise from under the covers. I'd know that noise anywhere! Never been so glad to hear the strains of the musical backside of my ball-faced mate! What a relief. Gave him a big hug

                    JACK
What the f! Get off you.

                    JIMMY

Thank Christ it's you. I thought maybe you and I had, you know....

JACK
Get lost, I wasn't that drunk not that I can't remember anything. You thought that we...

JIMMY
No, not you at first. I thought it was me and The Tea-cake.

JACK
What, I'm not good enough for you, is that it? I thought I looked good in this get up.

JIMMY
What?

JACK
If I saw myself dressed like this and I didn't know it was me, well, I'd definitely, you know.

JIMMY
You'd shag yourself? You're a freak, you still on the 'Smarties'?

JACK
What about you and Tea-cake, pot calling the kettle black there. Better not let Annie hear that, she'll cut your balls off.

JIMMY
Didn't happen, bloody Twiggy was at the wind up.

JACK
(to Georgy) So what happened last night?

GEORGY
The Tea-cake was going to break your legs.

JACK
And did he? (checking his legs) Scrub that!

GEORGY
Kept leaving the VIP lounge to look for you two.

JACK
Come again?

GEORGY

You were meant to deliver his bag, remember, but you were too busy enjoying his hospitality dressed like that.

JACK
Did Tea-Cake fancy me?

GEORGY
Come to think of it, aye, aye, he did.

JACK
(to Jimmy) There you go smart arse, told you I was an attractive woman.

JIMMY
But you're a man.

JACK
You know what I mean!

GEORGY
So, I bundled you both into a taxi, came back here.

JACK
Why, we were having a good time?

GEORGY
You were drugged out of your boxes.

JIMMY
We'd have been ok.

GEORGY
Christ, two minutes ago you thought you'd had it away with The Tea-cake! You would have been in major soapy bubble if I didn't save your backsides, <u>literally</u>.

JACK
We could have taken care of ourselves.

GEORGY
Well a wee update for you. Went back to the photo studio this morning. Couldn't get near the place, police everywhere.

JACK
What?

GEORGY
From what I could gather, some drug deal went bad, Terence, shot dead.

JACK
That'll stop his wandering hands!

GEORGY
Eastern European gang apparently.

JIMMY
Any news about my lucky scarf.

GEORGY
What do you think?

JIMMY
Just asking! (to Jack) This is all your fault, money, dressing up as women, getting propositioned, drugged, dead photographers, Eastern European gangs. And, worst of all, I've lost my lucky tartan scarf.

JACK
It's not lost, it was lying beside a dead body. It will turn up.

GEORGY
Aye maybe, once you're both arrested.

JIMMY
Even then, too late for the match.

JACK
We made £80.

JIMMY
(sarcastically) Worth every penny!

JACK
Do you always sleep like that?

JIMMY
Like what?

JACK
Your hands were everywhere, bad as that Terence. You men, only after the one thing.

JIMMY
Just as well you don't have the one thing then. There, there or there!

JACK
I'm going back to sleep, my head is spinning.

JIMMY

Good idea. Me too.

GEORGY
Eh, biggest Wembley ever?

JIMMY
Shit, the match, what's the time?

GEORGY
Just after one.

JIMMY
Get your arse in gear Diana Dors we've got a match to get to.

GEORGY
Don't forget Euston, the bag and your clothes unless you're going to the match like that.

JIMMY
Move it, can't be late especially this Wembley.

GEORGY
Aye, we know, biggest Wembley ever!

LX:	**Lights down**

VFX:	**Mellow Yellow by Donovan**

ACT 2 SCENE 3 – WEMBLEY, LONDON (14:50)

LX:	Lights up

OLD JIMMY (NARRATING)
Incidentally, that Mellow Yellow, found out a couple of years ago that an electrical banana was a vibrator! That Donovan eh, you can take the boy out of Maryhill but you can't take Maryhill out of the boy!

Finally got to Wembley ten minutes before kick-off. Had the bag. Managed to get Georgy in, slipped the guy on the gate a few bob. She'd never been to the football before, was a bit confused when we told her to jump over the turnstile but Jack was only too happy to give her backside a wee push to help her over. Wembley, what a match for her debut, just like Simpson and McCalliog but obviously much better looking!

We had bought some more drink for the match. Hopefully, the two dozen cans would see us through (pauses) to half time at least! We were at our usual spot, the barrier just down from the pylon.

GEORGY
Whoa, Abbot and Costello, thanks for waiting! All these stairs and me with my heels on, what was the hurry?

JIMMY
Last time we missed the kick-off we got a doing, not going to happen again, especially this year, biggest Wembley ever. Not that I'm superstitious!

OLD JIMMY (NARRATING)
I was very superstitious, still am (crosses his fingers).

Jack motions for Georgy to approach the crash barrier.

JACK
There you go, your own barrier, don't say that we're not good to you.

GEORGY
Where's my seat?

JIMMY

Seat, don't have seats, these are the ten bob tickets! This is our 'bit', just in front of the big pylon, we always stand here.

GEORGY
Aye, well I want a 'bit' with seats, what about they seats over there?

JACK
It's not the pictures, there's a hundred thousand people here. You can't just wander into a different 'bit'. They're about thirty bob they tickets, we're not made of money.

JIMMY
You mean I'm not made of money!

GEORGY
I'm not standing here for a whole hour while a bunch of dafties kick a ball about.

JACK
You mean an hour and a...?

JIMMY
An hour, you'll not notice the hour, it will whizz bye.

JACK
Plus half time, that's at least another ten...

JIMMY
Jack!

JACK
Then there's the singing after the game, that's at least another ten...

JIMMY
Jack!

JACK
Then when we win...

JIMMY
We might not win.

JACK
When we win, we'll not be leaving this place until they chuck us out. We'll be the new world champions and we'll not be moving. (singing) We shall not, we shall not be moved.

JIMMY
(to Georgy) There's the programme, have a read of that, tells you everything you'll need to know.

OLD JIMMY (NARRATING)
Was thinking that would keep her quiet for a wee while.

JACK
Look at that pitch, like a bowling green, could eat your dinner off it.

GEORGY
Speaking of which, I'm starving, can you get me a sandwich and a cup of tea, maybe a cake as well?

JIMMY
Tea, sandwich, cake! Christ, you're at the football.

GEORGY
And?

OLD JIMMY (NARRATING)
Had to explain about the lack of the most basic catering facilities, whereas nowadays you can virtually have a sit down meal at the football!

JACK
You're in luck, there's the spearmint chewing gum and macaroon bar guy. (shouting) Whoa, china, up here.

GEORGY
I need proper food! A macaroon bar?

JACK
It's food. (to Jimmy) Is it?

JIMMY
It's a small cake.

JACK
There you go, a cake, just what you asked for!

Jack goes to get the macaroon bars and spearmint chewing gums. Jack re-appears.

JACK
What a day for a match. Are you more confident now that we're here?

JIMMY

No!

OLD JIMMY (NARRATING)
Was always confident until I'm inside the ground then the reality hits and the nerves kick in.

JIMMY
It's going to be tough. Think we'll get a doing.

JACK
You always think we'll get gubbed. Why do you bother coming?

OLD JIMMY (NARRATING)
It was my in-built defence mechanism. Years of watching Scotland, I expected crushing defeats so I was mentally prepared for whatever happened

JACK
Can't be any worse than the 9-3 game.

JIMMY
No (thinks), aye it could, course it could. They could get ten, double figures, never been done before. The World Cup then taking ten off us, Christ!

OLD JIMMY (NARRATING)
Aye, the Samaritans would be on double time to cope with that.

JACK
Score prediction for a tanner? Four nil to the good guys.

JIMMY
Twiggy's been quiet?

OLD JIMMY (NARRATING)
Georgy was quietly reading the programme, my plan had worked, last thing you wanted, someone who's never been to a match asking you daft questions.

GEORGY
That's a shame.

JIMMY
Spoke to soon. What's that?

GEORGY
Missed the community singing.

JIMMY

The English, love their community singing, Abide with Me and all that shite. That's when we have our community singing.

GEORGY
Says here that if Scotland win the Home Internationals, they qualify for next year's Eurovision.

JACK
(sarcastically) I, we play Sandie Shaw, she doesn't wear shoes, even Nervous Nelly would fancy our chances against her!

JIMMY
What's it called again, show me the programme. (reading the programme) The European Championships, the Henry Delaney trophy.

JACK
That big fish shop at the top of Queen Street?

GEORGY
That's Henry Higgins.

JIMMY
More chance of winning the Henry Higgins cup!

JACK
Right, here they come. (shouting) "c'mon Scotland". We're going to win this one, no danger.

OLD JIMMY (NARRATING)
Huge roar, teams were coming out, this was it, no going back.

VFX:	Teams coming out the tunnel – ON

Something just got you when those teams emerged from the tunnel at Wembley. Looked around, took it all in, hands clapping, tammies, scarves, lion rampants, saltires. This was it. Jack and I hugged, we always hugged when the teams came out at Wembley, a tradition. Only time Scotsmen show any emotion is at the football.

JACK
This is it, biggest Wembley ever, we're going to do them.

JIMMY
Aye, we'll do them.

OLD JIMMY (NARRATING)

No, we wouldn't and I was shiting it, as usual.

VFX:	Teams coming out the tunnel - OFF

JIMMY

Here we go. (shouting) "Scotland". Who's the ref?

JACK

Guy in the red!

JIMMY

You need a new scriptwriter. Where's the ref from Georgy?

GEORGY

Eh, (checking the programme), eh West Germany.

JIMMY

Now we're cooking, he'll have no time for that mob, not after his lot were cheated last year. Any fifty fifties are ours, no danger.

JACK

Where's the Queen, is she not here? Who's that shaking hands with the players?

OLD JIMMY (NARRATING)

Bunch of guys in suits started shaking hands with the players.

JIMMY

No, can't see the Queen.

JACK

Aye, she knows her lot are going to get pumped, done a runner, couldn't take it, fearty. Queen's shiting it. This is our 9-3 game.

OLD JIMMY (NARRATING)

Was a little more less pessimistic. At this rate I might have convinced myself that we'd get a low scoring defeat!

GEORGY

(checking programme) Duke of Norfolk.

JACK

The Duke of Nor-<u>fuck</u>!

GEORGY

Who's he?

JACK
No idea, just like saying his name!

GEORGY
Does this happen before every match, players shaking hands with men in suits?

JIMMY
No, just the big international matches.

GEORGY
Why do they do that?

JACK
Well it's because, because, because, eh, Jimmy?

JIMMY
It's, eh, tradition. Aye, that's it, tradition.

JACK
Aye, tradition.

GEORGY
Do they shake hands at the start of the second half as well?

JACK
Don't be daft.

GEORGY
Why not?

JACK
Jimmy?

JIMMY
Because that's not a tradition!

OLD JIMMY (NARRATING)
Wait to you see this.

VFX: Scotland team line up - ON

OLD JIMMY (NARRATING)
See Baxter, standing a wee bit away from the rest, in a world of his own.

JACK

Look at Stanley, on his tod. Hasn't a care in the world, Slim Jim, what a player. He'll be wondering who won the 2:35 at Cheltenham!

GEORGY
Is that the skinny number ten with the blonde hair?

JACK
No, that's Denis. Number six is Slim Jim.

GEORGY
With the scruffy hair and the pot belly?

JACK
I'll 'pot belly' you!

JIMMY
No, she's right, he has got a pot belly. Christ, Slim Jim's got a pot belly! Well that's it, balls up on the slates now.

VFX:	Scotland team line up – OFF

JACK
Hurry up, for Nor-<u>Fuck's</u> sake!

JIMMY
For Nor-Fuck's sake.

GEORGY
'Sweary sisters', cut that out?

OLD JIMMY (NARRATING)
That was pretty tame compared to what she was going to experience. Think she was expecting something like a night at the pictures but the 'no seats' and 'no food' should have been a wee hint of what was to come.

A football match was nothing like the pictures. Can't explain why it's such a violent place or why everyone turns into an intolerant psychopath with Tourettes. Imagine going to the pictures, say to see Spartacus and when they did the 'I'm Spartacus' bit, the football equivalent would be some drunk punter would stand up and shout 'I'm fuckin Spartacus' then...

VOICE
Fuck off Spartacus

OLD JIMMY (NARRATING)

Fuck are you to tell me to fuck off, I'm fuckin Spartacus

VOICE
You're no fuckin Spartacus, come ahead.

OLD JIMMY (NARRATING)
Then a few more punters join in and before you know half of the pictures are on their feet, chanting, pointing "Spartacus, Spartacus get to fuck, Spartacus get to fuck". Well that's a football match (pauses) on a quiet day!

JIMMY
Shit, our kick-off, that's bad luck, Christ that's all we need!

JACK
You and your superstitions!

JIMMY
Big John must have won the toss, I'd rather have kept any luck for the actual match. Getting the same feeling I had at the 9-3 game.

GEORGY
(checking the programme) There's a coincidence, that 9-3 game was played on the same date as today, 15th April.

JIMMY
Nooooo!

JACK
Whoa, Nervous Nelly doesn't need any encouragement. Are you going to last the 90 minutes?

GEORGY
90 min...

JIMMY
60 minutes.

OLD JIMMY (NARRATING)
And just as we kicked off, these really big buggers stood in front of our barrier, couldn't see the pitch!

JACK
You're joking, whoa Gulliver move it.

JIMMY

Bloody typical!

GEORGY

What?

OLD JIMMY (NARRATING)

Was always the risk in they days, not like now in your all seated stadia with your unobstructed views. Those days there was always chance that some big buggers would stand in front of you, usually a few seconds before kick-off and you couldn't see the pitch. Big buggers, just our luck!

JACK

It's ok, I can see a wee bit of the pitch. (to Georgy) Here, can you give me those high heels in your bag?

GEORGY

What!

JACK

Don't have all day, it's an emergency.

OLD JIMMY (NARRATING)

Georgy had her modelling shoes in her bag, five inch heels, just the job. Jack and I took one each, this was better, get it right up you big buggers. Bit difficult balancing on the one foot so we put our arms around each other for support. (singing) We'll support you ever more, Bonnie Scotland.

Jack and Jimmy put on one high heel each, stood on their tip toes with their other foot and put their arms around each other and could now just about see the pitch. Georgy sat down as she couldn't see anything.

JIMMY

This is more like it. (shouting) Hit him Tam, hit him. Crunch. Big Tam, well in big man.

JACK

C'mon Scotland get a hold of the ball.

JIMMY

(shouting) Big John, yes. Well played Greigy. They just keep coming, somebody needs to get a grip of the ball. Where's Baxter? He's always bloody hiding when the other team have the ball. He needs to get his finger out his arse and get wired in. Told you, he's passed it, he's a liability.

OLD JIMMY (NARRATING)

Fans were in good voice, 'Scotland, Scotland' chants coming from all parts of the ground. About 50,000 of us. Christ, think about that number coming down from Scotland, we couldn't lose that game not with that support. Well, we could and probably would!

JACK

C'mon Scotland you're making this lot look good.

JIMMY

We're going to get a doing.

JACK

Calm down for Nor-Fuck's sake.

The guys join in the "Scotland, Scotland" chants with the Scotland supporters. Georgy looks on bemused.

JIMMY

Jesus referee, that big donkey Charlton nearly cut wee Bobby in half there, must be a booking. Dirty bastard!

JACK

Charlton's hurt . Hobbling off. (shouting) Serves you right you big donkey bastard.

GEORGY

His nickname is the giraffe.

JACK

Big giraffe bastard! Nothing, not even a talking to, so much for this referee being against them. So much for any 50:50s being ours!

OLD JIMMY (NARRATING)

We then started to dominate, they were virtually down to ten men with that big giraffe nutter hobbling about. Went close a couple of times, then it happened.

JACK

He's taking it off the keeper. Quick, in the middle, Denis. (shouting) Yesssssssssss, you beauty, the Law man.

OLD JIMMY (NARRATING)

Wallace nipped in between Banks and Cohen, crossed it, open goal, an open goal. Denis came flying through the air. A goal! It was bedlam and Jack and I fell off our platform shoes, didn't care, we were one up, one up.

					GEORGY
Was that a goal?

					JACK
Of course it's a goal, you beauty Denis, the Law man, get it right up you Ramsay.

					GEORGY
How come you're the only ones jumping about like a couple of dafties?

					OLD JIMMY (NARRATING)
Platform shoes back on.

					VOICE
Wanker Law. Fuckin sitter'.

					JIMMY
Open goal, I would have scored that, even wearing one platform shoe. Bloody Law, never rated him. Waste of space, hair like a lavvy brush. Should have been 1-0, we'll pay for that, we always do.

					JACK
There'll be more chances, just a matter of time. Playing well, told you. (shouting) C'mon Scotland. This is better.

					JIMMY
How many times is Baxter going to give the ball away? For Christ sake, that's the fourth pass that he's made an arse of. (shouting) Get your finger out your arse Baxter, clown, never rated you. Liability. Fuckin pot belly!

					GEORGY
How long gone?

					JIMMY
It's (realises he doesn't have his watch) I don't have my watch, my lucky watch. Where's my watch, Christ sake, that's all we need. We may as well go up the road, no lucky watch, no lucky scarf.

					GEORGY
It's only a watch.

					JIMMY

It's not <u>only</u> a watch, it's my lucky watch, big difference.

JACK
(checking his watch) Eh 26 minutes so just over halfway through the...

JIMMY
So that's almost half time!

JACK
What are you on about?

JIMMY
(nodding towards Georgy) Half time!

JACK
(nodding) Oh, aye, nearly half time.

JIMMY
Need a pee.

OLD JIMMY (NARRATING)
When I was really nervous, I needed to pee but in those days, packed in like sardines, couldn't leave your space to go to the toilet, never find your way back. When I say toilet, was actually a urine covered concrete wall at the back of the terracing. You'd usually just pee where you stood or the more considerate fan would use one of the many empty beer cans lying around.

So, empty can, I could feel the tension flowing out of me. Jack's bladder retention was usually much better than mine but with this being the biggest Wembley ever he asked for my can so I passed it to him when I finished, steam coming out of it. Zipped up, some tension gone.

But Jack was not as accurate as me, Georgy noticed a puddle under Jack's platform shoe.

GEORGY
Ground is all wet! Might be a burst pipe somewhere (she notices what Jack is doing). For Christ sake, don't tell me this is another one of your traditions, speak to him about that, it's disgusting.

JIMMY
Right, eh Jack. That's not on mate, it's eh, unacceptable that's what it is. That's what we have toilets for, we're not savages.

                              JACK

What!

                             JIMMY

There's a woman here, so, eh, let's stop this nonsense and don't let me catch you doing that again.

                              JACK

Because there's a woman here?

                             JIMMY

Aye, don't pee in a can if there's a woman here.

                             GEORGY

Don't pee in a can ever, no wonder you're single.

                             JIMMY

Aye Jack, unacceptable!

                              JACK

And what about you, you could pee in a can for Scotland? Bleeding William Tell of can pee'ers you are. Ping, right through the ring pull.

                             GEORGY

Well, get rid of it. Suppose I should be grateful you were only having a pee, I shudder to think what it might have been!

                      OLD JIMMY (NARRATING)

She needn't have worried about that, no one ever had a number 2 at the football in they days. If you couldn't last 90 minutes without needing a number 2 then you shouldn't have been at the football! Not like now with their cubicles, toilet pans that flush, toilet paper, soap and hand dryers, don't know they're born, football fans these days. In fact, with the effort the clubs have made, it would be rude not to have a number 2 at the football!

There is a massive roar.

VFX:	Denis Law celebrating - ON

                      OLD JIMMY (NARRATING)

Crowd behind us surged forward knocking me and Jack over and the can flew out of his hand. Unfortunately, some of the contents went over Georgy, she wasn't best pleased but never mind that, we must have scored, we must have scored, ya dancer. It was for real that time! She was collateral damage!

| VFX: | Denis Law celebrating - OFF |

OLD JIMMY (NARRATING)
Platform shoes back on and saw the pitch just as England kicked off.

JIMMY
Who scored?

VOICE
Scotland!

JIMMY
Bloody comedian. Who scored for us?

VOICE
Wallace.

VOICE 2
Gemmell.

VOICE 3
Denis, did you not see the arm in the air?

OLD JIMMY (NARRATING)
No public address announcer in those days to tell you who scored.

JACK
Denis, you beauty. Christ hen, what happened to your hair? (sniffs her hair) Not too keen on the smell of that shampoo!

JIMMY
Right, keep it tight. Slow it down. Nothing stupid Scotland. Just keep it tight, nothing daft.

JACK
We're all over them, should be three or four . C'mon Scotland, get into them.

JIMMY
All it takes is one mistake, one slip, awe, what, no, get it to fff...What a save Ronnie. That's what I mean, one is not enough, not against this lot.

OLD JIMMY (NARRATING)
Scotland fans were singing 'easy, easy' but it was still only one. Hate that chant, like tempting fate. Can imagine God sitting up there wearing HIS England scarf, thinking I'll give you fucking 'easy, easy'

Jock, bam equaliser, there's your dinner! But the 'easy, easy' chant finished without us conceding and the referee blew for half-time.

JACK
Hot Bovril Jimbo?

GEORGY
Hot Bovril, seriously, it's roasting!

JACK
Another superstition.

OLD JIMMY (NARRATING)
Women don't understand football superstitions, last time I didn't have my half-time Bovril was the 9-3 game, couldn't take that chance again. To be safe, I thought, better make it two, more Bovril's in the bloodstream the better and a pie of course.

JIMMY
Make it two.

JACK
Who needs a lucky scarf then?

JIMMY
Shit, shit, shit. I forgot about that, my lucky scarf and my lucky watch

JACK
Right, Bovril time, I'll be back when I'm back. Can you lend me a few bob?

OLD JIMMY (NARRATING)
Off Jack went and as Georgy was wiping away the last of the pish from her hair, I got a tap on the shoulder, shit.

TAM
Afternoon Jemima? And where is Jacqueline?

JIMMY
Eh, gone for a Bovril.

TAM
Bag?

JIMMY
There you go.

Jimmy hands over the bag and Tam unzips it and counts the money without taking it out of the bag.

TAM

A monkey short, hand it over, now.

JIMMY

A short monkey!

TAM

Stop fannying about, the monkey, now.

GEORGY

(to Tam) There's a policeman, call him over, he'll get your monkey back for you!

TAM

Stay out of this doll. Fucking polis. This isn't finished. I'll deal with you after the match, don't move from this spot and make sure you have that fucking monkey.

Tam walks off with the bag.

GEORGY

What was he on about?

JIMMY

Says Jack stole his monkey!

GEORGY

What would he want with a monkey?

JIMMY

Typical Jack, if anyone was going to do something as daft as stealing a monkey, Jack's your man! Bloody monkey thief!

GEORGY

He's taking his time.

JIMMY

Right, bad guys about to kick off. Feeling better with us shooting into this end.

Jimmy puts on one of Georgy's shoes.

GEORGY

Another superstition?

OLD JIMMY (NARRATING)

Know it sounds daft but always felt I could influence the players more when they were at my end of the ground. Defence played really well in the first half, clean sheet, wasn't just a coincidence, because I was nearer to them, kept an eye on them like. But I couldn't influence the forwards, at the other end that's why we only had the one goal. Second half, be able to keep an eye on the attack but I was worried about that defence too far away.

JIMMY
(shouting) C'mon Scotland, pick it up, don't let this lot back into it.

GEORGY
Hope he's ok, what if that nut-job has got a hold of him.

JIMMY
Shoosh, that's Ball again. (shouting) C'mon referee, whose side are you own? You're German, remember what this lot did to you last year, stole the World Cup. And remember what they did to you during the war.

GEORGY
What *they* did to them during the war!

JIMMY
(shouting) Ok, scrub the war, just remember what they did to your lot *last year*.

OLD JIMMY (NARRATING)
England had switched that wee niggle Ball to the left wing, he was causing problems, too many problems.

JIMMY
(shouting) Take it off that wee niggle.

OLD JIMMY (NARRATING)
He beat, one, two, three and squared it. I lost my balance in the excitement and fell off my platform shoe. A massive roar went up from the other end.

VFX:	England almost scoring – ON

JIMMY
Oh for f' sake they've scored, I told you, I told you, didn't I, one is never enough, not against this lot.

OLD JIMMY (NARRATING)

But the roar died down, stopped as quickly as it had started, maybe it wasn't a goal, maybe it was offside, no, this is Scotland, we don't get they kind of breaks. I got back on my platform shoe. Jack arrived back.

JIMMY
Have they scored?

JACK
No, the ball wasn't over the line, that lot thought it was but the linesman didn't give it.

VFX: **England almost scoring – OFF**

OLD JIMMY (NARRATING)
Turn up for the books eh, shoe on the other foot?

JIMMY
Get it right up you, the whole, bloody ball has to cross the line. (makes circling gesture) Nowhere near, clear as day. Thank Christ this linesman knows the rules.

JACK
There you go, two Bovril's, one a bit cold and one even colder! But here's a pie to make up for it. That's freezing!

JIMMY
Thanks. Took your time. Where's the monkey?

JACK
What would I want with a monkey?

JIMMY
That's what we would like to know. Just had a visit from that nutjob Tea-cake.

Jack realises the bag is missing.

JACK
The bag!

JIMMY
Tea-cake took it, said you've got his monkey, he's coming back at full time to get it.

JACK
What would I want with a bloody monkey?

JIMMY

He seemed pretty attached to it. Did you steal his monkey?

JACK
You've lost the plot. Let's go up the back, better view up there.

GEORGY
Better view than what, we don't have a view.

JACK
Higher up, get a better view of the goals we're shooting into.

JIMMY
Nutjob told us we've to stay here, he's coming back at full time.

OLD JIMMY (NARRATING)
Jack put on his platform shoe and we put our arms around each other and got back to watching the match.

JIMMY
Don't like the way this is going. Bit more even this half. They've upped their game, they've more of the ball, we need to get back to playing the way we did in the first half.

JACK
Relax, we'll do this mob.

JIMMY
Should have had a third Bovril, what was I thinking!

JACK
You'll be fine, I stuck one of they Smarties in your Bovril, that should calm you done.

JIMMY
What?

JACK
Found one in my hot pants this morning, they'll help you relax, make you feel mellow.

JIMMY
What! What! I don't want to feel bloody mellow.

OLD JIMMY (NARRATING)
There were a few chances for both teams but no more goals until...

JIMMY
How long?

JACK
Fifteen.

JIMMY
Fifteen minutes, that's eh (thinking) 900 seconds, 900 seconds. This is murder.

OLD JIMMY (NARRATING)
We were now playing better, we could see it out but we needed to slow it right down. Few minutes later we got a foul.

JIMMY
Slow it down, take your time. Don't take it quickly, for f' sake what are you doing?

OLD JIMMY (NARRATING)
It happened so quickly but then skelp, it was in the net. Bobby Lennox, we were two up.

VFX: Bobby Lennox celebrating - ON

OLD JIMMY (NARRATING)
The crowd surged behind us and we fell off our platform shoes but we didn't care, it was two, we were two up.

JIMMY
Ya dancer.

OLD JIMMY (NARRATING)
Two goal cushion and not long to go. Was feeling the most less pessimistic I'd felt all match. At this rate we might even get a draw!

VFX: Bobby Lennox celebrating - OFF

JACK
That's it, game over, they're not coming back from that. Easy, easy.

JIMMY
How long?

JACK
Twelve.

JIMMY

That long, that's (thinks) 720 seconds, that's ages. Right Scotland, keep it tight, tight, tight...Jimmy's voice tails off and psychedelic yellow lights appear.

OLD JIMMY (NARRATING)
Everything became a bit of a blur, just like the night before. That f'n Smartie!

JIMMY
Look at the sky, it's purple, why is the pitch white, why is the ball red?

JACK
On about?

JIMMY
Look at the size of the players' heads, they're massive man.

JACK
On about?

GEORGY
That'll be that Smartie you gave him. Here we go again!

JIMMY
Why are England playing in yellow with blue polka dots, why we playing in pink?

JACK
Scotland in pink! You've totally lost the plot now!

JIMMY
Love you mate, here, give me a kiss, but not on the lips, I'm engaged, Annie, she's my soul mate, have I told you that?

OLD JIMMY (NARRATING)
Georgy knew what to do, told Jack to throw lots of water in my face so he grabbed a few cans and whoosh, whoosh, whoosh. Amazing what a few cans of your own pish in your coupon can do to your faculties!

Wiped the pish off my face to hear our fans in full voice, 'Scotland, Scotland'. Just glad we were not singing 'easy, easy'!

JIMMY
What the f'!

JACK

Welcome back, what did I tell you, easy, easy?

JIMMY
Still 2-0?

JACK
Aye.

JIMMY
How long to go?

JACK
Ten.

JIMMY
Your watched stopped? Christ that's (thinks) 600 seconds. 600 seconds. A football match can turn in one second. One goal for them, we'd be in soapy bubble.

JACK
We want ten, we want ten. C'mon Stanley, stop taking the piss, we want ten.

OLD JIMMY (NARRATING)
Baxter had slowed the game right down, playing one twos at walking pace. Wasn't just taking the piss out of them, it was colonic irrigation!

JIMMY
Just keep the ball Stanley. They can't score if they don't have the ball.

OLD JIMMY (NARRATING)
Then England got it back. That wee shite Ball,

JIMMY
Somebody hit that wee shite.

OLD JIMMY (NARRATING)
Nobody heard me, too far away, so nobody hit the wee shite. Past one, past two, he was in the box.

JIMMY
Hit him, hit him, hit him, hit that wee shite, oh for f'sake. They've scored, they've fuckin scored. Fuck.

JACK
Consolation goal.

OLD JIMMY (NARRATING)

Aye, consolation goal if you're five up. We were going to balls this up, we always ballsed it up.

JIMMY
Christ we were two up, strolling about like we owned the bloody place, playing them off the park. One minute we're playing keep-uppy near their corner flag and less than a minute later they've scored. How long?

JACK
Six.

JIMMY
(thinks) 360 seconds, I can't take this. Told you to bloody hit him but nobody listened, nobody. Bloody typical Scotland.

GEORGY
Shame you're not wearing your lucky tartan scarf and lucky watch!

JIMMY
If, if, if you weren't a woman, so help me!

JACK
Relax, we're nearly there.

JIMMY
How long?

JACK
Four.

JIMMY
(thinks) 480 seconds, what, eh that can't be right, (thinks) 300 seconds, no, eh, eh, 240 seconds, that's right.

OLD JIMMY (NARRATING)
I was losing the plot,

JIMMY
They keep coming, we've blown this as fucking usual.

OLD JIMMY (NARRATING)
England sensed they could rescue the game but just as they were about to cross the halfway line, bang, wee Billy took the ball off Peters.

JACK

Well in wee man, brilliant. Keep going, its opening up. Give it to him, pass it, pass it.

JIMMY
No, for Christ sake, take it to the corner flag, waste time. Waste time, where are you going? Don't go towards goal. Into the corner, waste time Scotland, waste time. Into the bloody corner, for fffs sake...

OLD JIMMY (NARRATING)
Looked like wee Billy was following my instructions as he headed towards the corner flag. He was within shouting distance, he could hear me alright! But then from nowhere, McCalliog appeared at the edge of the box.

JACK
There he is, pass it.

OLD JIMMY (NARRATING)
Billy to Bobby to young Jim, perfect one-two with Wallace and the ball was in the net.

| VFX: | Jim McCalliog celebrating - ON |

JIMMY
It's in the f'n net 3-1, 3-1! You beauty.

OLD JIMMY (NARRATING)
This time Jack and I kept our balance, despite the crowd behind us surging on top of us and we saw the players celebrate. We saw Bobby Moore and Gordon Banks, they were on their arses, on their fuckin arses!

I didn't see the first two goals that clearly but I saw _that_ goal and every pass leading up to it, a thing of beauty so it was. Looked around the stadium, a sea of tartan, what a sight.

| VFX: | Jim McCalliog celebrating - OFF |

JIMMY
How long?

JACK
Three.

OLD JIMMY (NARRATING)
180 seconds, they were not coming back from that, were they, could they? Well of course they bloody could, this was Scotland after all!

JACK

We want ten, we want ten. Come on Scotland.

JIMMY

Right, now the corners, waste time. Kick it up here. Waste time. Tight, nice and tight.

JACK

Just for once, can you not just enjoy yourself?

JIMMY

(shouting) Shut him down, don't let him cross the bloody thing, shut him down...

JACK

Relax...

OLD JIMMY (NARRATING)

Bang, they'd scored, they'd f'n scored again, not even a minute after we'd scored.

JIMMY

Told you to bloody shut him down, but nobody could hear me, too far away. Bloody typical Scotland.

GEORGY

Who scored?

JIMMY

Who scored, well it wasn't f'n Scotland.

JIMMY

How long now?

JACK

Two.

JIMMY

Two! (emphatically) 120 seconds. I can't watch this (turns his back on the audience) 120, 119, 118...typical, bloody Scotland. 112, 111...

GEORGY

Counting backwards, that's impressive!

JIMMY

Told you at the start of the second half, have no control over that defence, they're too far away

GEORGY

Why do you keep shouting at the players?

JIMMY

What?

GEORGY

They're too far away, so why do you keep shouting at them?

JIMMY

Stupid question, I shout to help them, help the team, is that not obvious. Ok, they can't actually hear me because I'm a hundred yards away but I'm doing my best, trying to protect this lead. How long?

JACK

A minute.

JIMMY

(emphatically) 60 seconds. 60, 59, 58...nobody should have to go through this, it's inhumane. Aye, that's what it is, inhumane. We're going to snatch a draw from the jaws of victory, again.

OLD JIMMY (NARRATING)

Scotland, that is what we did best. If there was a cup for ballsing things up, we'd win that, every day of the week. Then it dawned on me that I'd never been to a football match with a woman before, that was it, it was her fault.

JIMMY

This is all your fault Twiggy, you're a jinx, a Jonah, a Jonah.—20, 19, 18...

JACK

Ignore him, always loses the plot. Nearly there.

OLD JIMMY (NARRATING)

And just as I could feel myself starting to hyperventilate, beep, beep, beep, it finished. It was finished.

JIMMY

Ya dancer.(turns around)

JACK

Dancer.

OLD JIMMY (NARRATING)

We had won. Jack and I hugged, we hugged everyone around us and Jack made a bee-line to hug Georgy!

We'd done it, we'd beaten that mob, in their 'ain midden'.

JIMMY
Always knew we'd do it, never doubted this Scotland team for one second, not one single second. Legends, all of them.

OLD JIMMY (NARRATING)
We'd done it and that was without the lucky tartan scarf and the lucky watch. Looked around, 50,000 Scots, what a sight. Jack and I hugged again and fell off our platform shoes.

LX:	Lights down

VFX:	Happy Together by The Turtles

ACT 2, SCENE 4 - WEMBLEY, LONDON (POST-MATCH)

LX:	Centre stage

VFX:	Fans on the pitch - ON

OLD JIMMY (NARRATING)
Thousands were on the pitch, so there was no holding us back.

VFX:	Fans on the pitch - OFF

JACK
There's Slim Jim, quick.

OLD JIMMY (NARRATING)
We could see Baxter, about twenty yards away. We were going to give Slim Jim a hug, a manly hug,

JIMMY
What a player, never doubted him for a second.

OLD JIMMY (NARRATING)
Jack wanted a bit of the pitch, for a souvenir so he got out his pen-knife. We were running towards Slim Jim, Jack waving his knife in the air! Just as we were a few yards from him, bam! Someone bundled Jack to the ground. Tea-cake.

TAM
Shouldn't play with knives, might hurt someone. Enjoy the match ladies?

JIMMY
Eh, aye. I thought we played well in the first half but then...

TAM
Shut it, monkey, now.

JIMMY
You see...

TAM
'You see', never like to hear those words. Monkey now or I'll make you pay for it, pay for it for the rest of your miserable, pathetic lives.

JIMMY
Look, he obviously doesn't have your monkey and why would you think we'd take a monkey to the football?

                    TAM
For the last time ladies, £500 now.

                    JIMMY
You want £500 and a monkey?

                    TAM
£500 is a monkey, idiot features, where is it?

                    JIMMY
Oh! Aye!

                    JACK
Someone stole it.

                    JIMMY
What?

                    JACK
Took it out the bag, had it last night but when I woke up this morning it wasn't there.

                    TAM
Right, had enough of this, think I'll need to take you two somewhere a bit more private, teach you a lesson.

                    OLD JIMMY (NARRATING)
The Tea-cake started dragging us away. I was really shiting it! Then Georgy caught up with us.

                    TAM
Not now doll, man's business, do you not have a nose that needs powdered?

                    OLD JIMMY (NARRATING)
Unbelievably, Georgy got the Tea-cake in a headlock, took the bag from him. I thought WTF as you kids say nowadays! Then she flashed a police badge.

                    GEORGY
Thomas Tunnock, I am arresting you for murder and also for the possession of Class A drugs and counterfeit money, anything you say may be taken down and used in evidence against you.

                    JIMMY
Twiggy is a cop!

                    JACK
Counterfeit money!

GEORGY
My colleagues are (pointing) there, there and there so I would suggest that you come quietly Mr Tunnock.

JACK
What a woman, I'm in love!

TAM
Wee fannies!

GEORGY
(to Jack) I'll need your full name and address for witness statements.

JACK
Like my phone number as well doll?

OLD JIMMY (NARRATING)
Jack gave her one of his special winks, aye that one, the one that looked like he was having a stroke.

GEORGY
Yes, please.

JACK
Don't have a phone, give you my next door neighbour's number, old Jessie. Call me anytime.

JIMMY
Do you not want my name and address?

GEORGY
It's ok, I have it here.

OLD JIMMY (NARRATING)
So, does she not produce my scarf, my lucky tartan scarf!

JIMMY
I knew it, just knew it. We wouldn't have won if my scarf hadn't been here.

JACK
So, you're not actually a model?

GEORGY
As if!

JACK
You could be, you're absolutely gorgeous. Not stopped thinking about you since we met. Fancy (pauses) going out for a (pauses) meal sometime?

OLD JIMMY (NARRATING)
So that would be me getting tapped again!

GEORGY
Well, thing is, how can I put it, you're not really my type.

JACK
Is it my bawface, cause I can suck in my cheeks?

GEORGY
No, it's eh, it eh...

JACK
Is it my clothes cause I can always get, eh borrow (looking at Jimmy) better clothes?

GEORGY
It's not that, it's just that , tell you what, I'll make you a promise, your daft pal thought Scotland were playing in pink, give me a call when that happens and we'll get together.

JIMMY
Nice knock back, well played Twiggy.

JACK
Scotland playing in pink, don't take the piss!

VFX:	Scotland players in 2014 wearing pink strips

LX:	Lights down

VFX:	Puppet on a String by Sandie Shaw

ACT 2, SCENE 5 – HORSESHOE BAR, GLASGOW (OCTOBER 2017)

LX:	Stage right

BARMAID

(shaking Jimmy) Old yin, wake up, time you were up the road.

OLD JIMMY

What, who, what, stop shaking me?

BARMAID

You've been sound asleep for the past hour and a half you dozy old sod.

OLD JIMMY

Rubbish, shut my eyes for a few minutes.

BARMAID

Few minutes! You were shouting and bawling about tea-cakes and Smarties and Snow White and pot bellies and...

OLD JIMMY

Away. (gets emotional)

BARMAID

Jimmy, are you alright?

OLD JIMMY

Aye hen, I'll be fine. (thinks) One of the greatest days of my life, beating that mob in the biggest Wembley ever. And Jack, what a laugh we had that week-end, although wasn't funny at the time!

(to audience) Was just dreaming. Shite. Thought it was real and I was 32 again. (holds up a small glass jar) This is Jack's piece of the hallowed Wembley turf. Wee bit of grass from a football pitch 50 years ago, one of my most precious possessions, daft eh? Well that's all I have left from that day.

Jack gone. My best mate. After my Annie died ten years ago, we only had each other, all our other mates passed away years ago. We were Bonnie and Clyde, Abbott and Costello! I've still got family, not that I see them much these days. My oldest turned sixty the other week. Christ, how could I have a sixty year old wean? Me, who doesn't feel that different to how I felt in 1967.

There's a point when you have to admit to yourself that you're old, that you're well into the second half of your life and heading towards the 90th minute so you hope that daft bugger with the big board is going give you loads of injury time. Thing is most of that additional time you will be injured and society doesn't have much time for the frail and the elderly, does it? Aye, the circle of life (pauses) it's pish! But I've still got the fitba, always have, always will. It's all consuming, an obsession, a disease but a good disease. It binds millions, billions of people together. We can't be all off our heads, can we? I'm going to miss him.
I mean he was a miserable sod, never spent a penny in his life, always tapping me but I loved him, loved him like a brother. Got a letter from his solicitor this morning, left me something in his will.

BARMAID
That bit of grass?

OLD JIMMY
No, I was expecting something like that but no, couldn't believe it. You see back in '67, he got accused of stealing a monkey.

BARMAID
A Monkey!

OLD JIMMY
It's a long story, a monkey is actually £500, but Jack always maintained that he did nick the monkey but somebody then nicked it from him. It was counterfeit money. Turned out he did nick it and bet it on Scotland to win and doubled it with Denis to score. Won eight grand the wee shite. Stuck it in the bank, never touched it. Too busy tapping me!

BARMAID
Must be worth a few bob now.

OLD JIMMY
Hold on (unfolding a letter) £152,928.33 to be exact!

BARMAID
Bloody hell!

OLD JIMMY
Aye, exactly.

BARMAID

But the bet was in counterfeit money, you can't keep it.

OLD JIMMY
Sorry hen, don't know what you mean, I'm just a simple old man!

BARMAID
Aye, a simple, <u>rich</u> old man!

OLD JIMMY
Here's something I thought I'd never hear, the drinks are on Jack! (lifts his glass) To absent friends.

VFX:	**Full Time**

END

VFX:	**We Fought With Law by The Tartan Specials**

Best team in the world, aye right! They needed to be put in their place so it's time to..

Bend it like Baxter

A play (rehearsed reading) by Jim Orr

19 November 2017
Kick Off 7:30pm
Tickets £10 (incl. Ticket admin fee)
Websters Theatre
416 Great Western Road,
Glasgow G4 9HZ

HOW TO BOOK
Online - www.webstersglasgow.com
email - boxoffice@cottiers.com
Phone - 0141-357-4000
In person - Websters Theatre Box Office

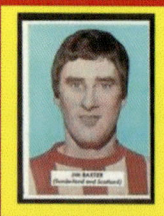

107.

FOOTBALL ASSOCIATION INTERNATIONAL MATCH

EUROPEAN CHAMPIONSHIP
HENRI DELAUNAY QUALIFYING TIE

SATURDAY, 15th, 1967

KICK p.m.

It's April 1967 and best pals Jimmy and Jack are on their way to London for the biggest football match of them all - England vs. Scotland at Wembley. As they head for the 'Big Smoke' their luck takes a turn for the worse. It's a 'trip' they'll never forget.

Bend it like Baxter is a comedy celebrating the 50th anniversary of the football match that Scotland fans voted the greatest ever.

England v Scotland

WEMBLEY

http://wembley67.co.uk/
https://www.facebook.com/benditlikebaxter/
https://twitter.com/the67trip

OFFICIAL PROGRAMME - - - - - ONE SHILLING

Bend it like Baxter

A play (rehearsed reading) by Jim Orr

It's April 1967 and best pals Jimmy and Jack are on their way to London for the biggest football match of them all - England vs. Scotland at Wembley.

As they head for the 'Big Smoke' their luck takes a turn for the worse. It's a 'trip' they'll never forget.

Bend it like Baxter is a comedy celebrating the 50th anniversary of the football match that Scotland fans voted the greatest ever.

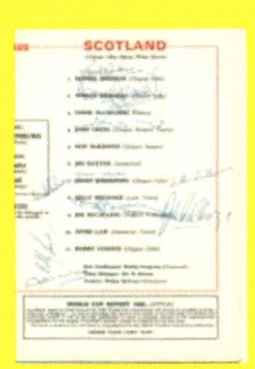

Scores from 1966/67

Celtic 2 Inter Milan 1
Rangers 2 Borussia Dortmund 0
Kilmarnock 2 Lokomotive Leipzig 0
Dundee United 2 Barcelona 0
Dunfermline 4 Dynamo Zagreb 2

...no really !!!

UFWC
Unofficial Football World Championships
All-time table as at 1 November 2017

RANK	TEAM	PLAYED	WON
1	SCOTLAND	148	86
2	ENGLAND	144	78
3	ARGENTINA	105	52
4	NETHERLANDS	82	50

Tonight's Players

Jimmy Chisholm — Old Jimmy
James Young — Jack 
Ryan Fletcher — Jimmy 
Matt Costello — Tam 
Michele Gallagher — Georgy 

Director – Jimmy Chisholm, Producer – Alyson Orr

Denis Law
(Goal No.1)

Bobby Lennox
(Goal No.2)

Jim McCalliog
(Goal No.3)

Bobby Brown
(Manager)

Rehearsed Reading - 19 November 2017

The cast with Jim McCalliog

Printed by Amazon Italia Logistica S.r.l.
Torrazza Piemonte (TO), Italy